THE ATLANTIS GUARD

BOOK 6 OF THE ATLANTIS SAGA

S.A. BECK

The Atlantis Guard: The Atlantis Saga

ISBN-13: 978-1987859515

ISBN-10: 1987859510

CONTENTS

CHAPTER 1

AUGUST 12, 2016, MARRAKECH,
MOROCCO
2:30 P.M.

Brice Dawson, alias Billy Conrad, alias Bill Carson, alias Malcolm Dryden, alias Grunt had been in a lot of bad situations before, but this one looked like it was going to be in the top ten.

He'd been prowling the backstreets of Marrakech, trying to sniff out what had happened to Edward, the computer hacker for the Atlantis Allegiance, and what he had found scared him. All his contacts in the underground—arms dealers, people smugglers, forgers, fences of stolen merchandise—all of them were afraid. In fact, most were so afraid that they wouldn't talk to him.

The only thing he had learned was that Edward had been snatched. The hotel/safe house Edward had found for them here had been attacked a few days before. The owner, Mohammad el Aoufi, had been gunned down, as had his son and several of the guests. The guests had included an important Italian businessman and a minor prince from the Saudi royal family.

El Aoufi's house was an underground institution, a supposedly safe refuge for all types of people who needed anonymity, and its destruction had made every criminal this side of the Atlas Mountains paranoid.

Everything had been hushed up. Nothing about the attack had made it into the local press, but no doubt the Moroccan secret police were scouring the medina looking for the culprits.

Grunt hadn't dared go near the hotel. The entire neighborhood would be filled with prying eyes. Instead, he'd heard all of this from the few people he could get to talk to him, quick whispered conversations at cafés while the contact looked the other way and hid his face behind a newspaper.

The underworld was in an uproar. One of their secrets, one of their safe spaces, had been taken out. The underworld was scared.

That made Grunt scared too.

All his instincts told him to get the hell out of Marrakech and preferably get the hell out of Morocco. Ideally he should get the hell out of Africa.

But he wasn't going anywhere. He had a duty to find Edward. He wouldn't leave a fellow soldier behind.

Grunt had one more hope, he thought as he looked at himself in the bathroom mirror of the tiny hotel room he'd rented for himself. The arms dealer, Ahmad Chukri, an old contact from his Special Forces days, had sent him a message through a go-between that he'd see him. For a price, of course. Nothing from that guy ever came for free.

First, Grunt had to get ready. He needed a disguise.

Checking into this hotel had been easy enough. This was the kind of place that didn't require a pass-port or even a peek behind the kaffiyeh he'd wrapped around his face. All he had to do was fork over some money and, to answer the question of why a foreigner would stay in this dump, buy some heroin from the guy at the front desk. The heroin had gone down the toilet as soon as he had gotten into his room, and the desk clerk had gone onto Grunt's Official List of People Who Needed Their Asses Kicked.

But that would have to wait for another day. He couldn't walk these streets without a disguise. Luckily he had that covered.

Grunt unzipped his toiletry bag and took out a tin of what looked like skin moisturizer. In fact it was a special chemical compound he'd learned to brew up.

Stripping to the waist, he dabbed the corner of a towel into the cream and began to rub it on the tribal tattoos that covered his face and neck.

A bit of rubbing and they came right off. Within a few minutes, the tribal tattoos had vanished, and the only ink he had left on him was his one real tattoo—the Special Forces tattoo on his bicep, a relic from an earlier part of his life. At least that was normally hidden by his shirt and couldn't be used to identify him.

Grunt examined himself in the mirror and smiled. The tribal tattoos were an improved version of the temporary tattoos to get in cereal boxes as a kid. While those faded after the first shower, his tattoos were drawn with a special ink that took weeks to fade under normal circumstances. But with his special cleaner, they came off like a charm.

He flexed his muscles and admired his reflection. The wrong side of thirty but still looking good. A faint scar underneath his Special Forces tattoo made him frown. That had been his only other real tattoo. He thought it would be there forever until he stopped being stupid and woke up to reality. Then he'd gotten laser surgery to rid himself of it. The tattoo had been only one word, once the sweetest word in the world and now something he couldn't say without spitting.

Isadore.

Grunt hurriedly put his shirt back on, so he didn't have to see the scar. Then he examined his reflection again, turning his head from one side to the other, making sure all trace of his tribal tattoos had vanished.

It was the perfect disguise. If someone has a tattoo on his face, everyone sees the tattoo, not the face. He'd been going around Marrakech with that facial tattoo the last time he was here. He'd bet a thousand bucks that the café idlers and the secret police and the street punks were still talking about the muscular American with the weird marks on his bald head, neck, and one-half of his face. Now he was just a muscular American. They wouldn't dream that he was the same person.

And that suited him just fine.

He slipped a Bowie knife into his boot and a smaller knife into a belt holster in the small of his back, wishing he'd had time to get a gun. If it looked like he needed to stay in town a while, he'd buy one from Ahmad Chukri.

Grunt closed the rickety door to his hotel room behind him, locked it for all the good that would do, and made his way down the dingy hallway, lit by a single bare bulb on which several dead flies were stuck. A cadaverous young Moroccan passed him in the hall, his hollow eyes barely registering Grunt's presence. It made the mercenary wince. He'd seen a lot of death and doled out plenty of it himself, but drug addicts had always given him the creeps. How someone could slowly kill themselves like that was something he'd never understand.

That thought made him briefly worry about Otto. How was the pyro doing, anyhow? He needed someone watching over him, and the eggheads weren't qualified. Vivian could handle the task, but she was too busy watching over Jaxon, which was more than a full-time job. That left Otto unsupervised most of the day, and that could lead to trouble.

The kid was an addict, plain and simple. Just as much of an addict as that junkie who had stopped in the hallway and stared at a couple of doors, obviously having forgotten which room was his. Otto was addicted to setting fires. Grunt reminded him of that every chance he could get in the hope that he could shame Otto into stopping. Otto cared way too much about what people thought of him, so that just might work. But without someone watching over him, it would be easy for the kid to slip back into his old ways or even worse ways. Addicts could change addictions easily enough, and North Africa offered no shortage of temptations.

Grunt passed down the creaky stairs, nodded to the guy at the front desk who recognized Grunt by his bulk rather than his face, which he now saw for the first time, and walked out into a narrow alley deep in Marrakech's medina—the medieval city that had stood almost unchanged for centuries.

Grunt took a long, winding route to get to Ahmad's place of business—visible from the alley only as a blank metal door identical to thousands of other blank metal doors in this private culture. Moroccans did not have windows open to the outside and never left their doors open for a second longer than it took to pass through them. Grunt knocked twice, then three times, then twice again.

A little window opened up in the door, covered on the inside by mesh so someone couldn't stick the muzzle of a gun through.

"I think you have the wrong place, tourist," a suspicious voice said in English. It was Muhammad, one of Ahmad's gunmen.

"Four sixteen," Grunt replied in Arabic. That was this week's code word.

Muhammad stared at him for a moment longer, obviously not recognizing him, then opened the door. He kept one hand hidden behind the door, no doubt with a gun in it, glanced each way down the alley, and let Grunt inside. When the door closed, Muhammad leveled a 9mm automatic at Grunt's stomach.

"Who are you?" Muhammad asked.

"An old friend of Ahmad's. He told you to expect someone at this time, didn't he?"

The suspicious look on Muhammad's face showed he still didn't recognize him.

"Go ahead," Muhammad said, gesturing with his pistol down a dark, narrow hallway.

Grunt sauntered down the hall, Muhammad following several steps behind to get a good shot and stay out of reach. Grunt smiled. Ahmad ran a tight ship.

Taking a right, they passed down another short hall and entered a large, brightly lit room with a couple of old couches.

Leaning on the couches and lined up on the tattered rugs on the floor were dozens of guns. Grunt eyed them appreciatively. Besides the usual AK-47 assault rifles, there were a variety of pistols, including tiny hideaway models that could fit in the palm of a hand, plus heavy machine guns from China and Russia.

A voice from the doorway opposite made him look up.

"Malcolm, my friend, how good of you to come visit!"

Ahmad Chukri the arms dealer came sweeping into the room, arms flung wide to make his white djellaba flow around him like some saint in a medieval painting. He paused for just a second when he saw Grunt's face free of any tattoos then smiled. He didn't seem the least bit surprised. Ahmad had risen up from a street punk to one of North Africa's leading arms dealers and had seen a countless variety of tricks, scams, and cons. Nothing surprised him anymore, not even a trick he'd never thought of. He nodded with the appreciation of one professional for another.

"It is good to see you again so soon. Come, let us have some tea."

Another assistant appeared from the doorway and set down a tray with an elaborate brass teapot and two little colored glasses. After the assistant left and Muhammad returned to his post at the front door, they drank their tea and got down to business.

"Thanks for letting me come over, Ahmad," Grunt said. "Most of my contacts are acting like I have the bubonic plague."

Ahmad made a face and shook his head. "Everyone is scared because of the attack on the secret hotel. We were all taken by surprise. Few people know of the place, and those who do appreciate its existence. I myself have put up many of my guests there. We all agreed it was neutral territory. We all benefitted from it, so we all honored its safety."

"You saying outsiders did this?" Grunt asked. Actually he already knew who did it—the hit had Isadore's fingerprints all over it—but he wanted local confirmation.

"Witnesses say the leader was a Western woman, but she had local help."

"What did she look like?"

Ahmad gave a vague but fairly accurate description of Isadore. Grunt nodded.

"And the local help? I thought you said people honored the place."

"Honored by professional people like you and me, my friend. Not street scum like the boys who did this."

Grunt reached into his pocket. "I don't have much time, so let's cut to the chase. How much for telling me where they are?"

Ahmad smiled. "Nothing, my friend."

Grunt stared. With Ahmad, everything cost, and cost a lot. The arms dealer chuckled.

"Are you surprised, Malcolm? We need to make an example of them. Come with us while we do this. You can question them and then go after their leader while we take care of the local boys. We cannot have such people ruining business like this."

"Let me handle the questioning," Grunt said. What people like Ahmad rarely understood was that torture was a poor way of getting information. The subject ended up telling their captors whatever they wanted to hear.

Ahmad spread out his hands and smiled. "Whatever you think best, my friend. You are a professional. But we get them when you are done. You know they killed a princeling of the Saudi royal family?"

"And you want the reward the Saudis will give."

Ahmad nodded. The smile on his lips belied by the hard glint in his eyes.

Grunt shifted in his seat. He didn't want to think what the Saudis would do to those street punks. Maybe he could find a way to save them, if they deserved saving.

"When do we move in?" Grunt asked.

"Right now," Ahmad said, picking up a pistol from the sofa and handing it to him.

CHAPTER 2

MUHAMMAD DROVE them and another gunman to a remote shantytown on the edges of Marrakech. Crumbling concrete houses stood along trash-littered dirt roads filled with potholes. Between the concrete buildings stood smaller shacks made of corrugated iron, wooden crates, even cardboard. Ahmad tut-tutted as he looked out the tinted windows of his car.

"It makes me sad to see my people living like this. The youth grow up with no respect, no culture. It is no surprise they act the way they do."

"Did you come from a neighborhood like this?" Grunt asked.

"Me? Ha! When I was young, I dreamed of living in a place like this. Look at those wires. There is electricity here, and running water in many houses. I did not have these things. I grew up in the

Rif, in a little village that you have never heard of. Oh my friend, people living ten miles away have not heard of my village. I have come far, and I will never go back."

Grunt shifted in his seat. He sounded like Isadore. When they had first met in the Special Forces, Isadore had still had an Appalachian twang to her voice she desperately tried to hide. One guy made fun of it once, and she decked him. That got Grunt interested. He started hanging out with her, going to the gunnery range and volunteering for missions he knew she'd be on. They admired each other for their skills and their eagerness to learn. Pretty soon they were an item.

At least for a time. Grunt began to find her drive a bit over the top. She constantly complained that the government didn't pay them enough and how one day she'd go independent and make more money.

"Why do you need money so much?" he had asked. "We get paid pretty good. They give us all we need, and we get to ride around in helicopters and blow stuff up in every part of the world. What else could you want?"

"You wouldn't understand, rich boy," she had said dismissively.

"Rich boy?" Grunt had laughed. "My dad was a bricklayer, and my mom was a waitress."

"You had shoes growing up," was all that she had said.

Grunt hadn't figured out a response to that.

In many ways, Isadore had been the ideal lover. She'd had the same sense of fun and was his physical equal. It was hard to find a companion who liked practicing at the gunnery range and parachuting out of low-flying aircraft into the jungle in the middle of the night. But there was a hardness to her, and a hunger. She'd never gotten over those rough early years. She was obsessed with money, even though she didn't seem to care about the things that money could buy. It was weird to lie in a lean-to made of sticks in the backwoods of some Third World dictatorship listening to her talk about how she was going to have a huge mansion someday, all the while knowing that she was perfectly at home in that lean-to. She was the kind of person who felt comfortable in rough places, just like Grunt did himself. She didn't want money for the things it could buy or even the security it gave. She wanted it as some form of power. Or maybe as a form of validation.

And that made her greedier than the richest oil baron or the most corrupt hedge-fund manager.

"Here we are." Ahmad's voice snapped him out of his reverie.

They stopped at the end of a rutted lane. A broken pipe had flooded a big stretch of it, leaving an oily pool. Several plastic bags floated on top. Ahmad pulled a 9mm automatic from his jacket and checked it. Grunt did the same with his.

"They are armed," Ahmad told him, "but we are more clever, my friend. We will surprise them," Ahmad said. He opened up a duffel bag that had been sitting at his feet and took out two police uniforms. After handing one to Muhammad, he began to get changed. "Their house is up there, the last house on the left. You and Mubarak will go along that other street you can see there and work your way around to the back of the house, where you will find another entrance. Keep out of sight and wait. I and Muhammad will simply walk down the street and knock on the front door, demanding entry. When they see us, they will make a break for it out the back door, thinking we are there to bust them for drugs. Then you catch them. Take care, my friend. They may be young, but they are quick and tough."

Grunt nodded. He and Mubarak got out, and the Moroccan hurried him down a small alley and then down a road parallel to the one on which the house stood. They saw few people around, mostly children and a couple of old women, the adults away for a long day of working or looking for work. The streets emptied as Grunt and Mubarak maneuvered behind the building. Grunt shook his head. In this kind of neighborhood, even the kids knew when a fight was brewing.

They passed through a small yard, where a little girl took one look at them and hurried her two goats inside. They heard her door slam as they made their way over a low fence to come to an open area littered with trash. The back of the target house stood before them. Two shuttered and barred windows and a metal door looked blankly in their direction. Grunt and Mubarak crept to the building and stood to one side of the door, drawing their pistols.

After a minute of tense waiting, they heard Ahmad and Muhammad pound on the front door.

"Police! Open up!" Ahmad shouted in Arabic. Grunt's Arabic wasn't all that good, but he understood that phrase well enough. He'd heard it a few times before.

There was a pregnant silence then another pounding on the door.

Suddenly a gunshot cracked the air. Grunt

ducked instinctively, even though his ears told him the fire came from the front of the house.

"These are very bad boys," Mubarak commented, not seeming the least worried. "You should not reply to the police in such a manner. It is very disrespectful."

Grunt stared at him. "Are you for real?"

He never got an answer to his question, because just then, a couple more shots rang out from inside the house. The back door burst open.

A teenaged Moroccan came running out. Grunt stuck out an arm and clotheslined him, catching him on the neck and knocking him flat on his back. His head smacked on the threshold, and he was knocked out cold.

The second teen out the door stumbled over his friend, then froze as Mubarak stuck a gun in his face. Grunt plucked a gun out of the kid's hand.

"All clear, my friend!" Ahmad shouted from inside the house.

They entered, the conscious teen carrying his knocked-out friend while Mubarak covered him. They found Ahmad in the living room, covering two more teens who lay face down on the floor, their hands behind their heads, fingers interlocked. One of them was bleeding from a flesh wound to the leg.

"Where's Muhammad?" Grunt asked.

"Checking the rest of the house," Ahmad replied.

Muhammad appeared a moment later. "No one else on this floor, but there's a cellar. Anyone down there?"

This question was directed at the teens on the floor and emphasized with a swift kick to the nearest one.

"No, there's no one. Are you really police?" one of them asked in a trembling voice.

"You're going to wish we were!" Ahmad laughed.

"Where's Edward?" Grunt asked.

One of the teens looked up. He was the oldest and appeared to be the leader. "You mean the fat American?"

"That's him, yeah."

His eyes got shifty. "We let him go."

Grunt picked him up by the collar and held him up. Their eyes met as the teen's feet dangled beneath him.

"What's your name?" Grunt demanded.

"Amir," the teen said, eyes wide with fear.

"Ahmad here is pretty pissed about you attacking Mohammad el Aoufi's hotel. And killing a member of the Saudi royal family? Nice work, dumbass. The

Saudis will give him a big reward for your hide. Lucky for you I'm around. You see, all I want to know is where Edward is, what you did to him, and who put you up to it. If you tell me all that and tell it to me straight, I'll let you and your buddies go."

Out of the corner of his eye, Grunt saw Ahmad stiffen. It was obvious that Ahmad had no intention of letting these punks go.

Grunt looked Amir in the eye. "I'm your only hope."

Amir's gaze shifted to the fake Moroccan policeman, to his friend lying wounded on the floor, and then back to Grunt.

"They will not kill me. I am CIA," Amir said.

Grunt thought that might actually be true; otherwise why would Isadore have picked these losers? Grunt shook him and bluffed, "Why shouldn't they kill you? No one knows we're here. Talk."

He could see the calculation going on behind Amir's eyes.

Then Amir told him everything—about Isadore and the American junkie she had with her, about the attack on the hotel, about questioning Edward. It took some more shaking to get the details of the questioning out of him. Grunt felt his stomach turn as the punk described badgering the frail recluse with noise and jabs until he had broken. Then Grunt felt fear well up in him to hear that, in the end, Edward had talked.

"He held out for a long time," Amir said. "He was a man in the end."

Grunt nodded. Good. There was that at least.

"And then you killed him," Grunt said. He had already resigned himself to this fact.

"No, the junkie did. Edward died of a heart attack."

"Where is he now?"

―――

The sun was setting when they got to the grave outside of town. They made the three street kids dig it up while the fourth one lay nearby, his gunshot wound wrapped with an old shirt.

The grave had been covered well, and the animals hadn't gotten to him. Edward hadn't been in there long, and Grunt could still recognize his face. He looked down at him in silence for a time.

Anger, sadness, and guilt. He felt all of those at once. He had always hated losing someone from his team. Even though it had happened more times than he could count, he never got used to it. Vivian had once told him that he shouldn't get used to it, that if he did, he'd become an animal like General Meade or Isadore. He supposed that was true, but he still dreaded these feelings.

"You were a good soldier," Grunt said to the body at his feet. "As good as any I've fought with. Rest in peace, my friend."

Grunt covered up the grave himself.

Once he was done, he turned to Ahmad. The arms dealer stood with his two assistants, guns aimed at the four street punks cowering on the ground.

"Amir here says they're CIA. If that's true, it would be a bad idea to kill them. Let them go," Grunt said in English so the teens wouldn't understand.

Ahmad shook his head. "The Saudis will give me a good reward. Besides, we need to make an example of them."

"But the CIA—"

Ahmad cut him off. "The Saudis will tell the CIA to choose their operatives more wisely. Nothing will come of this."

Grunt slumped. That was true. These young thugs were expendable. The government ground through people like them every day to achieve its ends.

"Don't give them to the Saudis. They'll torture them for weeks."

Ahmad shook his head. "I have no love for the Saudis. They sit rich on a big puddle of oil and let their Arab brothers live in slums. I will not give these boys to them alive to have fun with. Their bodies will be enough to get the reward. I will kill them quickly for your sake."

Grunt sighed. That was the best he could do. He took a last look at them. Amir looked back at him, pleading. So young.

Grunt shook his head. There was nothing he could do. This was why he had left government work. It always made him feel dirty.

And now he felt dirty again.

He turned and quickly walked away, but the distance he put between him and the gravesite did nothing to dampen the sound of the four shots that rang out one after another behind him.

CHAPTER 3

AUGUST 13, 2016, HEADQUARTERS OF THE
POSEIDON PROJECT, ALBUQUERQUE,
NEW MEXICO
11:45 A.M.

Things were going very well. With a lot of hard
work, a few necessary casualties, and a bit of luck,
he'd be dictator of the United States in a couple
of years.

General Arnold Corbin sat in the laboratory of
the Poseidon Project and watched Dr. Jones put the
two Atlanteans through their paces. Well, one and a
half Atlanteans. Orion was a true Atlantean that his

colleague General Meade had kidnapped and mentally enslaved through hypnosis. He was in tip-top condition and, with some more training, would be an efficient killing machine. Even now he was punching through bricks better than any triple black belt. General Corbin had to step back to avoid getting hit by the fragments.

General Meade himself was the other subject. The fellow had discovered too much about General Corbin's plans and had had to be neutralized. Killing a general of the United States armed forces would lead to an investigation, something Corbin certainly didn't need at the moment, so Corbin had come up with a better plan. His scientists had produced a serum that, theoretically, would give regular humans the powers of Atlanteans. Or, theoretically, it could kill them. Luckily for everyone involved, it had actually worked. Disposing of a dead general was not something Corbin was prepared to do. Yet.

By all appearances, General Meade was still the same person he had always been—a fit middle-aged man whose muscles and posture showed a lifetime of healthy living in the military. But now he could bench press four times his own weight and run as fast as an Olympic sprinter. His mind wasn't the same, though.

Where once there was a sharp, perceptive intellect, there was now the mind of a lazy slob, begging to be told what to do and having no initiative whatsoever.

It was ironic, General Corbin thought, that he was taking over America to get rid of such human trash, and in the process he'd had to create someone just like the people he hated.

Oh, but not for long. His hypnotist was working on General Meade to redevelop his mind. A true soldier had to take orders but also had to be able to think for himself. Besides, General Meade couldn't stay on sick leave with a "bad case of the flu" forever. Sooner or later, he had to return to his office and discharge his duties. He'd be the perfect secret agent in the Pentagon to develop Corbin's plans.

And those plans were nothing short of ruling the United States.

Democracy had failed. The system was only as good as the voters, and look at the voters! A bunch of weak civilians who had never been tested in war, who expected everything to be handed to them. Fat, lazy, addicted to television and the internet, these weren't the kind of people who had made America great. They didn't deserve the vote.

They deserved to remain the sheep they had become, led by someone strong. Not the big corporations that were wheedling their way into every corner of power in the nation. They only looked out for their own interests and were largely responsible for the dumbing down of America through a steady bombardment of mind-numbing media and advertising. No, the nation needed a strong military leader, someone who could set the country back on the right course. Someone who would get the people trained up to be the great fighters they had been fifty, a hundred years ago. Someone who could lead the nation back to supremacy over the world.

That someone was himself, of course.

General Corbin had studied the dictators of the past and knew that he needed three things to gain power—an external threat, an army loyal only to him, and chaos in the civilian government.

The external threat was easy enough. For years he'd planted stories of UFOs in the civilian press and had even faked some top-secret documents that had convinced many members of the government and military, including General Meade. Those false stories had grown ever more ominous. Anyone gullible enough to believe in aliens would think there was an invasion coming soon.

The loyal army was coming along nicely too. His research team was perfecting the serum so that it could be put into mass production, and with the help of an expert and entirely unscrupulous hypnotist, those new Atlanteans would obey his every word. One was being tested in the field right now.

Brett Lawson had gone to Morocco with his agent, Isadore Grant. If Brett worked out well, then Project Poseidon could start mass production. General Corbin was already thinking of ways to get a large number of subjects to supply his army. They had to be people who would not be easily missed. He could always abduct active-duty soldiers in places like Afghanistan and Iraq and put them down as missing in action. No, he mused, that would take too long, and he couldn't abduct too many without the Pentagon noticing a rise in MIA numbers. Homeless people? No, too many of them were sick or mentally ill or substance abusers. That might affect the process. So who? It was a tough problem, but he knew he'd find a solution.

The third factor he needed to grab success, chaos in the civilian government, was developing all on its own. The two political parties had always sniped at each other, but in the past decade, that had descended into a complete lack of cooperation. It seemed like nothing could get done anymore beyond the basic functions of government and sluggish responses to the most obvious external threats. General Corbin was developing a new propaganda team alongside the one that spread his UFO misinformation. This team, codenamed Operation Bicker, would spread so much negativity about politicians in both parties that no one in the civilian government would look credible. Luckily there was plenty of real material to use if one knew where to dig, but Operation Bicker would also make things up.

It had already sent out some test stories about a few members of Congress who seemed likely presidential candidates in the next election. One story claimed a senator from Texas was a member of the Ku Klux Klan. Actually his grandfather had been, but little details like that didn't matter. It was guilt by association. Another story had a congresswoman from New Hampshire cheating on her husband with a member of the Russian Mafia. She'd studied Russian in college, so there was enough of a hint to create a line of nonsense implicating her in something she had never done.

The trick was to make things sound believable. That Texas senator had said a couple of nasty things about Black Lives Matter, and with his grandfather's association with the KKK, enough people would believe the fake part of the story to seriously hamper his chances at running for president. A doctored photo of that congresswoman showing her in the arms of the Russian mobster was good enough to go viral. She could deny it all she wanted, but it would still be shared and reshared all across the internet. Hardly anyone checked what they saw on that network of lies.

That was the big advantage of trying to take over a lazy and ignorant nation—he could make them believe anything. He didn't need everyone to believe it all, just enough people to make those who knew the truth waste most of their time and energy trying to stamp out the lie.

Soon he'd have hundreds of these credible lies clogging up the internet so that no one would be able to tell the difference between truth and fiction anymore. Project Bicker would make the American people turn on one another and make them too divided to stop him when he made his bid for power.

And no one outside of his inner circle knew a thing about it.

No one, that was, except the Atlantis Allegiance. Luckily they thought General Meade was still in charge. They didn't know about him or his real plans at all, but Meade's goals had been close enough to his own that they knew far, far too much.

They had to be eliminated.

That was proving difficult.

An assistant came up to him as he watched General Meade run 30 miles per hour on a treadmill without breaking a sweat.

"I thought I said I didn't want to be disturbed," General Corbin barked.

"You said only in the case of an emergency, sir," the assistant said.

"So I did. Well, what is it?"

"Your contact in the CIA called. Those local operatives in Marrakech, the ones Mrs. Grant was working with, they didn't check in tonight like they were supposed to."

General Corbin rubbed his chin. All operatives had to check in on a regular basis whether they had something to report or not. Those particular local contacts, while just a gang of teenage street thugs, were proud of their role in the world's largest intelligence agency and had always been punctual.

"I suppose the CIA is looking into it?"

"Yes, sir."

"Keep me informed."

"Yes, sir," the assistant said and left.

General Corbin knew they wouldn't be found. Isadore had been sloppy and had killed too many people to capture Edward. A couple of them had been important, an Italian heroin wholesaler and a minor member of the Saudi royal family on a secret pleasure holiday. While the world would be no worse off for their deaths, it was causing ripples. Someone must have killed those street kids out of revenge, not knowing they were affiliated with the CIA.

But who? And would this imperil the mission? What if the young crooks had talked?

Then he thought of another possibility.

What if Edward had gotten a message out before he was taken? Hackers were clever, and he had been a damned good one. What if someone from the Atlantis Allegiance had come back to Marrakech to check on him, found the teens, and rubbed them out?

That meant he'd have a chance to grab them while they were isolated from the rest.

He moved into an office he'd had set up in the lab, closed the door, and pressed the buzzer on his desk to speak with his assistant.

"Who do we have in Marrakech?"

"No one, sir, but the McKay twins are in Tangier, just a quick flight away."

General Corbin shuddered. Even on the other side of the world, those two gave him the creeps.

"What are they doing there? Are they on a job?"

"No, sir, they're on vacation."

"Why would they vacation in Morocco? Wait, don't tell me, I don't want to know. Send them in. Find, question, and kill."

"Usual fee, sir?"

"Usual fee," General Corbin sighed, shaking his head. Taking over America was proving to be expensive. He needed to work on some more income streams. There was only so much he could skim off his government budget.

He leaned back in his chair, lacing his fingers together on his stomach and thinking. Yes, the more he considered it, the more likely it seemed that some of the Atlantis Allegiance had come back to Marrakech.

He'd looked at the files on those street punks. They were smarter and more careful than the usual kids in their position, which was why the CIA had chosen them in the first place. Plus there were several of them. Even if one or two had been killed in some robbery or been picked up by the local police, always an occupational hazard when using criminals, the others should have still made their regular report. They'd never missed before.

So who had it been? Grunt or Vivian? Perhaps both?

No, not both. As far as he knew, they were the only muscle the Atlantis Allegiance had. One would have stayed behind in Timbuktu.

Both were tough and would be hard to catch, but the McKay twins would be able to run either of them down.

Oh yes, no one was a match for the McKay twins.

Not Grunt, not Vivian, not even Isadore.

CHAPTER 4

AUGUST 13, 2016, HOTEL CARAVANE,
TIMBUKTU, MALI
3:15 P.M.

Otto Heike should have been happy.

Two months before, he had been in prison and had just run out of money to bribe his fellow inmates not to beat him up or worse. He had been facing a long stretch for an arson he had, for once in his life, not committed, and he had no hope that anyone was going to save him.

Now he was on the other side of the world with a beautiful girlfriend in an exotic locale and having the time of his life learning about guns and explosives from a mercenary who had shown him more care than his negligent parents ever had.

At least in theory. At the moment, all he could do was curl up on the lumpy mattress of his bed and make occasional runs to the bathroom to shoot toxic liquid out his backside or his mouth or sometimes both ends at the same time.

To make matters worse, his girlfriend, Jaxon Ares Anderson, was hardly ever around. She'd finally found her people and had been talking with them nonstop for the past couple of days. Of course, that had been the whole point of the Atlantis Allegiance making a dangerous trek across the Sahara in the first place, but it left Otto feeling alone and useless.

It didn't help that Grunt had flown off to Marrakech to search for the computer hacker of the group, leaving Otto with no one to confide in. Jaxon was convinced it was a pointless mission. She seemed to sense that Edward was dead. That made Otto feel even worse. Jaxon's intuition generally turned out to be right. She'd found that healing spring in the middle of the desert, after all.

He wished he could drink some of that water now. It would cure him instantly. They didn't have much left, though, probably only enough for one seriously injured person, and the way people got hurt in this group, he knew he couldn't waste it on something as minor as a bad case of food poisoning.

Lying on the bed and looking up at the cracked concrete ceiling, Otto tried to count his blessings. At least he wasn't in jail, and at least he wasn't completely alone. Doctors Yuhle and Yamazaki looked in on him every few hours to check how he was feeling and give him some medicine, and that medicine was finally beginning to work. He spent more time in bed now than sitting on the chipped bowl of the toilet (no toilet seat; this was Mali) hoping he wouldn't keel over and expire. People cared about him in this group, but he couldn't help feeling a bit left behind when everyone went off to do something cool.

After his tenth trip to the bathroom that day, Otto realized he was beginning to feel a bit better. Instead of running to the toilet every half hour or so, he'd made it a whole fifty minutes this time. He decided to dare a trip down the hall. He was getting cabin fever being stuck inside like this all day.

The Hotel Caravane wasn't much to look at. The hallway was grubby, with cracked plaster on the walls and no decoration. It had no other guests than the Atlantis Allegiance. There had never been much tourism in Timbuktu, but after a terrorist group called Al Qaeda in the Islamic Magreb had taken over the place for a brief time a few years ago, tourism had stopped completely. Otto wondered how the hotel had managed to stay in business.

A Malian in his early twenties sat at the front desk, his feet propped up on the counter and a battered old radio in his lap playing desert blues through a tinny speaker. Otto remembered that amazing night with the Tuareg rebels in the desert, sitting by the campfire eating camel as they played steel guitars under the stars. His life sure had gotten interesting since running away from America.

"Hey man, feeling good?" the Malian said.

"I'm not dying, anyway," Otto replied.

The guy flashed a peace sign. "Bob Marley."

"Um, yeah, Bob Marley to you too."

Otto decided to step outside and get some fresh air. The hotel was too dark and gloomy.

As soon as he got out, he appreciated dark and gloomy. The hot Saharan sun hit him like a sledge-hammer, and its glare made him stop and blink, momentarily blinded. He'd been in the desert for a couple of weeks now, but he still hadn't gotten used to it. He wasn't sure he ever would.

Shadowing his eyes with his hand, he looked up

and down the street. It was pretty quiet at this time of the day. Even the locals preferred to do most of their work in the early morning or late afternoon when the sun wasn't so brutal. A man led a string of donkeys carrying some sort of plant in big bags. Another stood haggling at the salt stand just down the street. Salt stands were something he'd never seen before coming to the Sahara. Big slabs of pressed salt that looked like marble floor tiles stood in tall stacks in front of the owner, with more leaning against the building behind him. Salt was precious here and came on the backs of camels over the desert. Dr. Yamazaki had bought a big chunk of salt and mixed it with sugar and water, telling him to drink some of the mixture every hour to rehydrate himself. Being sick, he had to make sure to replenish his salt as much as he needed to replenish his fluids.

Directly across the street stood a clothing stand. A man in a peach-colored djellaba and a white skullcap sat cross-legged on a reed mat, putting some bright-green cloth through an antique sewing machine. Surrounding him were stacks of brilliantly colored cloth. Some were decorated with abstract designs that dazzled his eye as they shone in the sun, while others showed simple pictures of camel caravans or leaping gazelle.

Otto had some money in his pocket and suddenly got an idea. He'd surprise Jaxon with a gift! He touched his stomach nervously. It seemed to be all right. At least his room wasn't far off. He could sprint back to safety if he needed to.

He went over to the tailor, who nodded at him and said something in Arabic, spreading out his hand to invite him to browse. Otto nodded back at him. He really needed to learn the local language. Only being able to speak English made him feel like an idiot. Every African he'd met spoke at least two languages, usually three or four.

He stared at the cloth, picking some samples up and examining them while wondering what Jaxon would look like dressed in the different colors. The tailor got up and held a bright-red cloth to Otto's chest, saying something in an approving tone.

"Oh no, it's not for me," Otto said. "It's for my girlfriend. Um, you have no idea what I'm saying, do you?"

The tailor seemed to understand the word "no" and figured Otto didn't like the color. He put the red cloth down and picked up a deep-blue one, the color of the Tuareg.

"No, you see, it's for my girlfriend."

A flow of Arabic came from behind him. Otto turned and stared.

An incredibly beautiful European woman in her mid-twenties stood behind him. She wore loose green robes in the local style but had a bulky camera bag slung over her shoulder, worn hiking boots on her feet, and mirror shades hiding her eyes. A green headscarf shielded her head from the sun and covered the hair as was traditional here, although a stray blond lock had broken free to blow in the desert wind.

The tailor replied to her in Arabic, and Otto stood silently as they exchanged several sentences, occasionally gesturing at him.

Now he felt even more like an idiot. Whoever this was spoke Arabic like a pro, and here he was standing there tongue-tied.

At last the woman turned to him.

"So what kind of outfit does your girlfriend want?" Her voice sounded as lovely as she looked and had what sounded like a Russian accent.

"Um, I'm not really sure. It's supposed to be a surprise, and I don't have her measurements."

The Russian woman gave him a smile that made his knees tingle. She lowered her sunglasses to reveal startlingly bright green eyes.

"Surely you must know her measurements by heart?" she asked.

"Um..."

She laughed. "It does not matter. Perhaps you can get her a headscarf. Is she Muslim?"

"No."

"Then you should know her measurements by now," she said, wagging a finger at him as if he were a naughty schoolboy. "Do not worry, all women need a headscarf in this climate. See, I have one. It keeps the sun off the head and the sand out of the hair. I will help you pick one for her."

"I'm Otto," he said, extending his hand.

"Jaxon's friend, I know," she replied, taking it. When Otto blinked in surprise, she laughed again. Those laughs were wonderful. They made him feel like he was floating on air. Otto needed to think of some jokes, fast. He wanted to hear that laugh again.

"Are you surprised?" she went on. "This is a small town, and foreigners are rare since the terror attacks. I am Nadya. I am friends with Dimitri Rublev. Do you know him?"

"Oh yeah, the guy who works in the manuscript museum."

"He spends too much time there with his dusty old books instead of spending time with me," Nadya said as she looked through the different lengths of cloth.

Otto didn't know what to say to that, so instead he asked, "So what do you do here?"

"I am a photographer. This is a rich place to take photographs. It helps that I am a woman, one of the few advantages to being a Western woman in a Muslim country. It puts them at ease. I can take photos inside houses and of women. Do not try to take photos of these things yourself. It will insult them."

"I don't have a camera with me," Otto admitted.

Nadya looked up from the cloth. Otto realized he had made a mistake.

"A tourist without a camera?"

"It got lost in a sandstorm while we were camping in the Sahara."

That was half true. His phone and iPad got lost that way, which had included the only cameras he owned.

Nadya shrugged. "I think green or red would look good on her. She is one of the People of the Sea, yes?"

"You know about them?" Otto asked, surprised.

"Oh, they are part of the folklore here. Very photogenic, but they do not like having their pictures taken. You know they say all sorts of silly things about them? Some say they have magical powers."

"I've never been superstitious," Otto said.

"Oh yes," she said quickly, "just superstition. Your girlfriend is not casting spells on you, is she?"

"No," Otto said, chuckling.

She cast a cool spell on that Mauritanian cop, though, Otto thought. *Made plants sprout up right out of the ground and grabbed him like a lasso. He's probably still having nightmares about that little trick.*

Nadya held up an emerald cloth with gold thread running through it. "I think this will work. It will contrast nicely with her dark skin and bright eyes."

"Thanks. I'm not good at this stuff."

"Men are useless at such things. But where is your girlfriend? Why are you not with her?"

"I'm kinda sick," Otto admitted. He didn't like to tell her that, but if he had to suddenly sprint for his hotel room, he needed some excuse. He wouldn't want her to think he was ditching her. No, definitely not.

"Oh, poor you," Nadya said, putting a hand on his cheek. "The food does not agree with you?"

Otto blushed, both from the contact and from her knowing that he had screaming diarrhea.

"Do not be embarrassed, Otto. It happens to us all in this part of the world. You are not going to run off on me, are you?"

"Not at the moment."

"Good," she said brightly. "Because I like your company. If you need to run off for a minute, do not be shy. It is better that you leave me for a short while than you have a little accident in your jeans, eh?"

Otto blushed again.

Nadya said something to the shopkeeper, who had been standing patiently nearby, and he took the cloth from her hands. Within a minute, he had cut and sewed it into a perfect scarf. A quick bit of haggling and Otto handed over the equivalent of three dollars.

"A bit overpriced," Nadya told him, "but life is hard here, and it is all right if they charge us a little much."

"Seems like a good deal to me."

"Come," Nadya said. "You can buy me a tea. There is a little café on the corner."

Otto looked uncertainly at the front door of the hotel.

"Oh, come on," she said, taking his hand. "It will

be good for you to get out. You must be bored staying inside your hotel room for two days."

Otto wondered how she could have known that. Oh well, he must have mentioned it. Tucking Jaxon's scarf under his arm, he followed Nadya down the street, both of them sticking to the narrow slice of shade cast by the buildings.

The café was a little adobe building no different from all the others. It had no sign, and the only way to tell it was a café was that the front door was open, something you never saw in a private residence.

Inside was a dim little room with a few scarred wooden tables and some rickety chairs. In one corner sat a silent trio of Tuareg men, lifting their indigo veils to sip their tea without showing their faces. Their people were the reverse of all other Muslims, with the men covering their faces and the women going unveiled. At another table sat a couple of Malian men in Western clothing having a loud conversation while studying an Arabic newspaper.

Nadya chose a table away from the talkers and sat down. All eyes followed them, although the two men with the newspaper hadn't stopped talking.

Otto had gotten used to being stared at in this part of the world, but he realized that what really caught their attention was the sight of a woman sitting in a café. That wasn't done anywhere south of Marrakech, and not so much even there. Nadya didn't seem to care, and when the waiter came, a skinny kid of no more than fourteen, she ordered some tea in her fluent Arabic.

She pulled out a packet of Camel cigarettes.

"Smoke?" she said, offering them to him.

"I don't smoke."

"Smart boy. It is a bad habit. Do you know the story of Camel cigarettes, why they are called this?" she said, holding up the packet to show the image of the camel with a pyramid and a few palm trees in the background.

"No."

"Back when they started business a hundred years ago, Egyptian tobacco was considered the best. The Americans put a camel and a pyramid on their Virginia tobacco to make it look Egyptian."

"I didn't know that."

"The Americans steal a lot from this region, as do the British and the French. The Russians, we give."

Otto wondered how true that was but couldn't think of a polite reply before getting distracted. Nadya put a cigarette in her mouth, lips pursing slightly. She pulled out a gold Zippo lighter, flicked open the top, and lit it. A long, steady flame danced before him, brilliant in the café's dim interior. The flame made Nadya's green eyes sparkle, the fire reflected in both of them looking like a vein of gold within an emerald. Otto gasped at the beauty of it.

Nadya held that pose for what seemed like an eternity. At last she leaned a little forward, a little closer to him, and touched the end of her cigarette to the flame. The tobacco crackled and shone like a little coal. Otto shivered.

Nadya snapped the Zippo shut. Otto jumped a little.

"You are interesting," Nadya said, looking into his eyes.

"Me?"

"How old are you?"

Otto was tempted to exaggerate his age, but something in her steady gaze told him that he wouldn't get away with it.

"Eighteen."

"Aha! I thought so," she said and put a hand on his. "This is why you are interesting. You are so young. Of course I am young too. I am only twenty-eight. I suppose this makes me sound old to you?"

"Not at all," Otto replied, his throat going dry.

"I am at the age when one is expected to be doing interesting things. For years I have been a photographer. I have gone all over the world. But you, you are doing the same thing at an age when most people are stuck in a dull classroom."

"I, um, dropped out. The traveling life seemed more interesting to me."

Nadya nodded appreciatively and squeezed his hand. "And that makes you interesting. When I heard such a young man had come all the way from America to visit Timbuktu, I said to myself, 'Here is a man I want to meet.' I am happy to say I am not disappointed."

Otto couldn't believe his ears. Was this stunning woman really interested in him?

Suddenly he felt guilty. What would Jaxon think if she saw this? He pulled his hand away. Nadya didn't try to hold on.

The tea came, and they spoke of their travels in the Sahara. Nadya had been in Timbuktu for some time and appeared interested to hear of his adventures through the desert, asking for all sorts of details about the trip. Otto was careful what he revealed but gave her a long description of the sandstorm. She nodded and listened with rapt attention. That made Otto feel good.

Jaxon won't mind this, he told himself. *All we're doing is talking.*

If all you're doing is talking, why do you have to justify it to yourself?

"So where else have you worked?" Otto asked.

Nadya shrugged and blew out a long stream of smoke. "Chechnya, Syria as a war correspondent. All over America. My favorite was Hawaii. Have you heard of Volcano National Park? There is lava that flows into the sea. You can walk very close. The most amazing colors. Plus I went to the rim of a live volcano and looked down at the bubbling lava far below."

"Wow."

"They are beautiful photos. I will show them to you. They are in my room."

Otto's eyes widened. "Your room?"

"It is not far."

Otto's stomach gave an ominous rumble. He knew that sound all too well. Nadya's gaze flicked down, and a smile stole across her lips. She put a hand on his knee.

"I think you need to go. Will you hurry back?" she asked.

"Of course."

She gave his knee a squeeze. He had meant it before. Now he meant it twice as much.

"I better go," he said, his mouth going dry.

Nadya Antipova watched as that silly American boy hurried out of the café with the stiff-legged walk of someone suffering from a bad case of food poisoning. It was incredible that such a fool had made it so far. It was as she and Dimitri had suspected. He was the weakest link in the chain of the Atlantis Allegiance. She had practically hypnotized him with that lighter trick. Stuck here more or less alone in Timbuktu as the more capable members of his team were off doing something useful, he was ripe for the picking.

She pulled out her cell phone and wrinkled her nose to see there was no signal. Mobile coverage in this part of the world was always unpredictable. Even the smallest building often blocked it. She walked to the door, and her phone showed a weak signal. She dialed.

"Yes?" a curt male voice replied in Russian.

"How are you progressing with your scientist friends?" she asked.

"Well enough."

Nadya smiled. Dimitri was nothing if not cautious. They must be in the room with him, and even though they almost certainly spoke no Russian, he wasn't about to say anything that might give him away.

"I met with the young man we spoke about," Nadya said.

"Did that work out?" Dimitri asked.

"Like a lamb to the slaughter. No, more like a moth to a flame."

Nadya hung up and went back to her table with a smug smile.

CHAPTER 5

AUGUST 13, 2016, TIMBUKTU, MALI
8 P.M.

Jaxon Ares Anderson was the happiest she had ever been. For the first time in her life, she felt like she belonged. For the first time in her life, she felt like she was safe.

She sat in the front room of the home of Daouda Ndiaye, a famous griot, or storyteller, of the Atlanteans. The room was thickly carpeted, and everyone sat on the floor, leaning against yellow and green cushions set against the wall. About thirty people had assembled there, all with the broad Asian faces, dark skin, and sparkling blue eyes typical of her people.

For years, those features had set her apart. White people called her black, black people told her she wasn't "really" black, and Asians didn't know what to think. Everyone had been in agreement, though, that she wasn't "one of us."

America claimed to be a "melting pot," she thought bitterly, but when she showed them a melting pot, everyone rejected her.

What she didn't know until a couple of months ago was that she wasn't of any race known to mainstream science. She was a descendent of the people of the lost continent of Atlantis, and thus a member of her own distinct race. Or perhaps the race that had given birth to all the others. Not even her fellow Atlanteans had the answer to that riddle.

The scientists Yamazaki and Yuhle were at the local manuscript museum studying historical records with a Russian scholar named Dimitri, so Jaxon was able to enjoy a rare moment alone with her people. The Atlanteans—or People of the Sea, as the locals called them—were uncomfortable around outsiders, so with the prying scientists gone, everyone felt much more relaxed.

The old Atlantean griot Daouda Ndiaye wore a

flowing green and gold djellaba that set off his long white beard as he sat cross-legged on a cushion with an old handwritten manuscript on his lap. Jaxon had never seen him without a book open in front of him. Even when deep in conversation, he managed to glance at the pages every now and then and read a few lines. She'd already learned so much from him about her people's history. Next to him sat Salif Amar, a younger man dressed as usual in a spotless white djellaba. He had been the first Atlantean she had met in Timbuktu and had made it his job to introduce her to everyone.

Jaxon sat between two women. To her right was Hawa Ndiaye, Daouda Ndiaye's granddaughter. She was in her twenties, a teacher in the local school, and one of the few people Jaxon had met who could speak good English. Snuggling up on her left was Aminata, a girl of eleven who lived next door and who had instantly decided that Jaxon was her long-lost big sister. Somehow they managed to have long conversations with Aminata's broken textbook English and Jaxon's few words of Arabic.

Everyone except Jaxon wore the flowing traditional robes of Mali, all brightly colored. The women all wore headscarves, and most of the men wore skullcaps. Jaxon still dressed in the Western style with jeans and a T-shirt. It was so hot outside that she felt like walking around in a bikini, but this was a conservative society. She'd have to get some local clothes. They looked much cooler.

At the moment, Aminata and Jaxon were trading vocabulary words. The kid felt like it was a wonderful game and never seemed to tire of it.

"*Gafsha*," Aminata said, holding up a spoon.

"*Gafsha*," Jaxon replied in a pretty good imitation. "Spoon."

"Spoon?" Aminata giggled. For some reason, she found that word funny. Jaxon wondered if it meant something else in Arabic.

Tea came, as tea always did in this region, on a big brass platter holding a giant gleaming teapot and a collection of little colored glasses. Mariam Ndiaye, the griot's wife, brought it in. Jaxon couldn't even begin to guess how old she was. Her dark face was as dark and seamed with wrinkles as a walnut, but her hands remained steady and strong. As guest of honor, Jaxon got the first cup, along with a cube of sugar to set between her teeth. She loved drinking tea this way, but she'd have to watch it. A lot of the older people in this part of the world had pretty bad teeth. Mariam Ndiaye didn't have any teeth at all.

"*Shukran*," Jaxon said.

"Thank you," Aminata translated.

"Exactly," Jaxon said and tickled her. As the girl giggled, Hawa Ndiaye put a newspaper in Jaxon's lap.

"Look at this," the schoolteacher said.

The newspaper was in Arabic, a mass of squiggly lines that meant nothing to Jaxon, but Hawa was obviously telling her to look at the photo. It showed a group of families walking through the desert with bundles on their backs. They looked like refugees. On the left edge of the photo, she saw a family of Atlanteans.

"What does this article say?" Jaxon asked.

"It's about refugees from Mauritania," Hawa replied. "It says that hundreds more refugees have fled the fighting in the past month and crossed illegally into Mali."

"Does it say anything about us?"

Hawa shook her head. "No, it just talks about the refugees in general, but it's good to see one family got out."

Jaxon bit her lip. They'd crossed through Mauritania to get here and had heard that the government was rounding up all the People of the Sea. No one seemed to know why, and Jaxon and her friends weren't about to ask the government.

They'd barely gotten out of that country with their lives.

"We need to bring them here, where they can be safe," Jaxon said.

"They're already safe once they got across the border," Hawa said, sipping her tea, "but it would be better for them to be among their own kind."

"What if they get kicked back over the border? They're here illegally, right?"

"The article says the government in Bamako will let them stay."

"What's Bamako?"

"The capital of Mali!" Aminata laughed. "You no go to school?"

Jaxon blushed. Yeah, she had been to school. But her school never got around to talking about Africa. To cover her embarrassment, she asked, "Have any of our people from Mauritania made it all the way here?"

"No," Hawa said. "The refugees left with nothing. Many got robbed on the way. They have no way to get here. Right now they are in a camp at Ras el Ma, a village near the border."

"Is it far? We should go get that family and any others who are there!"

Aminata nodded. "I go too."

Hawa translated her idea to the rest of the group, and this started a long discussion in Arabic. As usual, Jaxon felt frustrated when everyone started speaking in a language she didn't understand. It made her feel stupid, and she had been made to feel stupid all of her life because of her dyslexia.

It took some time to get a translation of what was going on, and when she did get it, Jaxon didn't like what she heard.

"We would like to help, but there is the problem of where to put them and how to support them. They are getting some help in the camp, but if they leave, the government won't help them. And there is little work here."

"My friends and I can support them until they find work," Jaxon said. Thanks to Edward's activities on the Dark Net, they had plenty of cash, although it wasn't going to last forever now that Edward was gone. "We can use the two Land Rovers to pick them up."

This led to more discussion. Finally Daouda silenced them and turned to Jaxon.

"This is very generous of you. Let us get it arranged. But I don't want you to make the same mistake as many kind Americans and Europeans make."

"What's that?" Jaxon asked.

"Thinking that money can solve all life's problems."

"I don't think that!" Jaxon objected.

"You might think that you do not, but you have been raised with that as part of your culture. I have seen Western channels on the television. It's all advertisements. Even the shows are advertisements. They tell you that if you have enough money, every-thing will be all right. Some problems can't be solved with money but only with wisdom and cooperation."

For the first time, Jaxon felt a bit annoyed by this kindly, welcoming man. Here she was offering to help and all she got was a lecture?

She brooded for a time, letting the conversation go on around her without really hearing it. After a while, Aminata nudged her and started their word-trading game again. Jaxon put on a smile and helped the girl with her English.

Later that afternoon, Jaxon met with the rest of the Atlantis Allegiance at the Caravane Hotel. Yuhle and Yamazaki had spent the entire day at the manuscript library looking for legends about the People of the Sea. Vivian had been working on the Land Rovers, which had taken a beating on their overland journey. Otto had spent the day recovering in his room. At least he looked a bit better.

They all met in Vivian's room.

"I'm glad you were fixing up the Land Rovers, Vivian," Jaxon announced. "Because we need to go on a road trip. Some Atlantean refugees from Mauritania have ended up in a village near the border called Ras el Ma."

Vivian checked the topo map. She traced a slim figure west from Timbuktu across a long, thin lake to a point on its western shore, where a tiny dot bore the name Ras el Ma. "It's only about 150 miles from here. A long day's drive on these roads, but we can make it easily enough. It's a bit too close to the border for my liking, though."

"We can't just leave them there!"

"I'm not saying that we should, honey," Vivian replied, her blond hair swaying as she shook her head. "It's just that with Edward having disappeared and Grunt away, I don't think we should split up any more than we already have."

"We'll all go together," Jaxon objected. "We won't be splitting up."

Dr. Yuhle adjusted his glasses and said, "I'm afraid we'd have to split up. Otto isn't well enough to travel yet, and someone has to stay and monitor his progress. I suggest I stay, since Yamazaki is a much better driver than I am. That chase through the desert was better than an amusement park ride. I felt like I was twelve again."

He grinned at his colleague, who chuckled.

"I don't think any of us should go until Grunt and Edward come back," Vivian said.

Jaxon sighed. Edward wasn't going to be coming back. When she had been half dead, she had seen a vision of him. He was gone. She didn't know what had happened to him, but he was gone.

His last words to her haunted her.

Make this mean something.

She would.

"I asked the folks at Daouda Ndiaye's house today, and they told me there's a bus that goes there. I can go myself, if you don't want to."

She decided to leave out the detail that the bus only left once a week, stopped at every village in between, and took eighteen hours.

"Absolutely not! It's too dangerous!" Otto said. "I won't let you."

"That's not for you to decide," Jaxon snapped.

Vivian smiled. "I can see where this is leading. You always end up winning these arguments, so all right, honey, we'll go. We should find out what's going on in the country next door anyway. It might clear up why General Meade has been chasing us so much. But we're going to do this intelligently. Yuhle will have to stay here with Otto. The rest of us will go. We'll leave before dawn so as not to attract too much attention. Tell your friends that we have to go down to Bamako for some of Dr. Yamazaki's research."

"What's Bamako?" Otto asked.

"It's the capital of Mali. Didn't you go to school?" Jaxon laughed.

Her boyfriend rolled his eyes and didn't reply.

Jaxon blew him a kiss and turned back to Vivian. "I don't really want to lie to my new friends about where I'm going."

"It's for their own protection as much as ours," the mercenary said.

"I agree with Vivian," Dr. Yamazaki said. "She knows more than us about these things. We have to work as a team, Jaxon. The scientists handle the science, and the mercenaries handle security."

"And what do I handle?" Jaxon said.

"You're the reason we're out here in the first place, honey," Vivian said. "Plus your instincts seem to be pretty good. Remember that well? Don't worry, I'm trusting your instincts from now on."

"All right, but my instincts tell me not to lie to the other Atlanteans. I'm not sure they'd believe me anyway, because I was already talking about going to collect the refugees. How about this? We'll just leave without saying where we're going. If anyone asks, Otto and Yuhle can say we'll be back in a day or two and not volunteer any more information."

"All right," Vivian said, although she didn't look happy. "Let's start getting everything ready. We'll leave first thing tomorrow. The sooner we get this over with, the better."

Everyone filed out into the hallway and split up to go to their own rooms. Jaxon noticed Otto looked down.

"Hey, I was only teasing about Bamako. I just learned that. I suck at geography too."

Otto shook his head. "It's not that. It's that I feel like a fifth wheel around here. They busted me out of prison to help convince you to run away, but now what good am I?"

"Oh come on, you've done plenty!" Jaxon said, although she couldn't actually think of anything. Still, it was nice to have him along.

They walked down the dark corridor for a moment in silence. As they made it to Otto's door, he brightened.

"Well, I know one thing I'm good for. Hold on a second."

He went into his room and came back carrying a scarf of emerald cloth with gold thread running through it.

"Wow, this is beautiful!" Jaxon gave him a hug and a kiss. "Where did you get it?"

"From that guy across the street. I think it will look good next to your skin and eyes. Really bring them out."

"You sounded like a fashion designer for a second there," Jaxon said and laughed. "Did someone help you pick it out?"

Otto got a strange, guarded look on his face. "No."

Jaxon felt confused for a second and then brushed it aside. The poor guy was still sick and depressed.

"Well, you have a good eye for fashion. Thanks. I'll wear it on my trip to meet the refugees."

Otto gave a sad little shrug. "At least I'm good for something."

CHAPTER 6

AUGUST 14, 2016, MARRAKECH,
MOROCCO
11:30 P.M.

Grunt had been right—this really was turning into one of the top ten most messed-up situations he'd ever been in. Lying in a filthy Third World alley covered in bandages and suffering from internal bleeding was something he'd experienced a few times before, but this time, it felt personal. Usually when an enemy got the better of him, it was in some anonymous fight in which they just happened to be on different sides.

But a secret faction within the US government was out to get him and his friends in particular, because they were the only ones opposing what General Meade was up to. One side was so much smaller than the other.

Even that hadn't bothered him too much. He'd been in unequal fights before. It was just that he was failing against the one man he'd sworn to defeat. That bastard—General Meade, his former boss—had won.

Grunt eased himself into a sitting position. Lying flat on the ground would only attract the rats, both human and rodent. Pain lanced through his body as he moved. He gritted his teeth and shifted the few inches to the alley wall and forced himself up. The cuts on his body and the deep wound in his side tortured him. He kept his left hand pressed against the worst wound. His right hand gripped a length of pipe he'd scrounged somewhere. He couldn't remember picking it up. It was his only weapon, and he didn't have the strength to swing it, but he could still bluff with it.

His mind ran through the events of the past thirty-six hours. Where had he gone wrong? People got hurt in the field through either miscalculation or bad luck. Which had it been for him?

After Ahmad and his men took care of the boys who had killed Edward, they had driven back to Marrakech in silence.

"You should not feel badly about them, my friend," the arms dealer had said when he dropped Grunt off in town. "They killed one of your men and killed many a good man in the hotel as well."

When Grunt hadn't responded, Ahmad put a hand on his shoulder and squeezed. It was an unusually intimate gesture for someone who made his living selling death.

"You feel bad because they are young? I feel bad too. But think of it this way. As soon as they burst into neutral ground and started killing people, they had taken their own lives. They were fools to do this. Soon enough, someone else would have killed them. That is the law. And do you think whoever else did it would have been so kind as to give them a quick bullet to the back of the head? No, my friend. They would have suffered too much. And imagine if the Saudis had taken them! They would have lived for many terrible weeks."

Grunt shrugged. Everything Ahmad had said was true. Not that it made any difference to how he felt. He'd become a soldier because he wanted to be a warrior. As a kid, he'd devoured stories of chivalric knights and noble samurai. He'd dreamed of becoming an honorable fighter defeating evil in the world.

It hadn't worked out that way.

His first fight had been Operation Desert Storm, the move to push Iraqi leader Saddam Hussein out of Kuwait. That was pretty straightforward. Evil dictator takes over another country. You go in and kick out the evil dictator. Fair enough.

The bombing of the Iraqi cities hadn't been too cool. He had tried hard to ignore the reports of "collateral damage." He had tried hard to ignore the reports of smoke billowing from exploded oil wells and the Euphrates River becoming radioactive from the spent uranium rounds fired by the American A-10s. Instead he focused on the happy Kuwaitis cheering as their country was liberated. He got good at focusing on one thing and not another.

Things got trickier when he joined the Special Forces. He'd done well in Desert Storm and had applied for the military's most prestigious fighting unit. He passed the training with flying colors and found a girlfriend in Isadore and a best friend in Vivian and plenty of fellow warriors to fly around the world and kick ass with.

Most of his missions had been against targets the

public had never heard of. One was a drug kingpin in Central America who had just come up with a new highly addictive and ultimately fatal drug. They'd gone in and wiped out the lab before the stuff could make it to the streets. Another target had been an international arms dealer who had gotten his hands on some plutonium and was trying to sell it to the highest bidder. After wiping the guy's bloodstains off his computer and checking his files, Grunt's team had discovered a list of the highest bids. The names and nations there had given Grunt nightmares for weeks.

Then they'd gone into North Africa to hunt down a radical Islamic group called the Sword of the Sahara. By then, Isadore had left to start her "free-lance" career, and Grunt was nursing a broken heart. When General Meade offered him the mission, he'd leapt at the chance. A bit of action in a remote corner of the world always made him feel better.

He had thought it strange that the general had asked him to go instead of ordering him.

"I only want volunteers for this mission," the general had said by way of explanation. "It's going to be tough."

It had been. The Sword of the Sahara had gotten onto the US government's hit list because it had good funding from various sources in the oil-rich Gulf States and could afford to attract the best fighters in the region. The shadowy powers that started and funded radical groups all around the world had finally gotten serious. Instead of just throwing some money at some wild-eyed hicks with guns, they'd built the foundation for a proper army, complete with highly trained fighters and sophisticated weaponry like surface-to-air missiles. Luckily it was just in the beginning stages. It was the job of Grunt, Vivian, and their team to nip it in the bud.

What General Meade had failed to mention before they burst in on the group's camp in the middle of the night, guns blazing and tossing incendiary grenades, was that the jihadist fighters had brought their families with them.

A woman and three small children went up in flames right in front of Grunt's eyes. He had been responsible for that.

By the time the team had figured out what was going on, it was too late to stop. The terrorists were fighting back, and all the innocent people got caught in the crossfire.

That night, the Sword of the Sahara was wiped out, at the cost of a couple of hundred innocent lives.

General Meade congratulated them on a mission

accomplished. Grunt and Vivian resigned from the Special Forces.

So as Grunt lay dying in the alley, he looked at the balance of his life and wondered if it had been a force for good like he had intended or if he'd screwed up royally. Yeah, the Sword of the Sahara fight had stained his soul forever, but on the other hand, he'd stopped the sale of enough plutonium to make three ICBMs. Any one of the people on that buyers' list would have used it. He'd saved a hell of a lot of lives in that mission.

So okay, on the whole, the balance was positive. But that didn't feel good enough.

Because he'd failed at his latest mission.

After Ahmad had dropped him off back in Marrakech, Grunt had purchased a new cell phone and a SIM card so that he couldn't be traced and tried to call Vivian to warn her that Isadore was on her way. But he'd been stymied by the region's poor cell phone coverage. He couldn't get a connection with Mali. He tried a few times but still couldn't get through.

So he'd gone to an internet café and sent a coded email. Both of them had set up anonymous email accounts. It was simple enough. Edward had explained the whole thing when they had first formed the Atlantis Allegiance. First, you avoided the big names like Gmail and Yahoo, which kept meticulous records on all their customers and sold that information to advertisers. Instead, you went for the privacy-based ones set up by hacktivists in places like Switzerland and the Netherlands. But even these required you to give a backup email where the server would send a confirmation code, so sooner or later, you'd have to give a name, right? Luckily, there were several free services like EmailonDeck that gave you a one-shot anonymous account through which you could receive the confirmation code.

Once that was done, you had yourself a truly anonymous email account. And as long as you used it in internet cafés, no one could trace you. Grunt had to admire Edward's brains. He was a mess physically, but he thought like a warrior.

So Grunt went to an internet café and sent a coded email warning Vivian of the danger.

That part of his mission done, his next step was to get back there and help out. He was frustrated to see that he couldn't get a flight until the day after tomorrow, so he had booked one and sent another coded email telling Vivian when he'd be back.

Then he'd gone back to his hotel room to get some well-earned rest.

The next morning, he checked out and moved to another hotel, both for safety's sake and also to have the satisfaction of kicking the owner's ass for selling heroin to vulnerable junkies. Then he robbed him and distributed the money to beggars—all women with children—on his way to find a new hotel. This time he picked one that wasn't a haven for drug addicts. If he kicked a new hotel owner's ass every morning, he'd develop a bad reputation.

Grunt didn't sleep well that night. Memories of those burning families kept flaring up in his mind. At times, when he was just drifting off to sleep, he'd jerk awake, thinking he'd heard shots. Then he'd slump back in bed, knowing that was just his conscience playing tricks on him.

As the muezzin made his lilting call for the dawn prayer, Grunt got up. He was stuck in Marrakech for another day with nothing to do. He hated inactivity. After two hundred pushups and two hundred sit-ups and a cold shower, he felt a little better. He found an internet café that opened early and checked for Vivian's answer.

Instead he found a message from his anonymous email account.

"UNABLE TO DELIVER MESSAGE DUE

TO PRONY RELAY ERROR. COULDN'T CONNECT TO THE RESET BN SERVER."

What the hell was that supposed to mean? When faced with this sort of gobbledygook, he missed Edward more than ever. It took fifteen minutes on Google to figure out that Mali had blocked the email server he was using. It took another hour and some puzzling through a French computer magazine's webpage to find out why.

Just two days before, Mali had blocked a long list of anonymous email servers. Their stated reason was to "combat terrorism," which in this part of the world meant "suppress political dissent from the tribes we're oppressing and combat the types of terrorists we personally don't support."

Grunt rubbed his chin. Edward had warned him that these email servers sometimes got blocked. A lot of people who wanted to guard their privacy used them—including political dissidents and members of various armed groups. Mali's ban on the email account could just be to block actual terrorists—the country had no shortage of them, after all—or it could be targeting some other group.

The timing made him suspicious, as did a mention on one news site that this had been done as part of an American antiterrorism plan. That plan had included "extra funding for local security forces." A bribe, in other words.

General Meade and his shadow government in the States knew the Atlantis Allegiance was in this part of the world. Isadore's presence proved that, and Meade was deeply embedded in the antiterrorism section of foreign relations. Could he have guessed they'd be using anonymous accounts and instigated this just to hurt their communications? Or was it simply an unlucky coincidence?

Whatever. The main thing was that he couldn't warn Vivian. He'd keep trying on the phone, which was risky because it could be located via the cell phone relays, but it appeared all their attempts at secrecy had been blown anyway. Hopefully he'd get through. And if he couldn't, hopefully his silence would keep Vivian on her toes.

Worse was waiting for him when he got back to the hotel.

His hotel, although much better than the fleapit he'd stayed in the night before, was still a pretty run-down place on a narrow side street deep in the medina. Few foreigners came to that neighborhood, and those who did came looking for trouble. So anytime he saw one, Grunt would give them a quick once-over and size them up.

The man casually strolling along the street just outside his hotel made him look twice.

He appeared English, with the bony white skin, pale blue eyes, and blocky features of someone from a Northern industrial town, Birmingham or Manchester or some smaller place. His hair was shaved within half an inch of his scalp, and his face bore countless little scars that showed he had been in plenty of fistfights. The English, especially the working-class English, liked a good fight, and this man's stocky body and thick arms, disproportionately long like a gorilla's, hinted that he would be good in one. He wore scuffed black dress shoes, black pants, and a buttoned-up white dress shirt, completely inappropriate clothing for summer in North Africa. He looked like a waiter in some cheap restaurant.

He also looked like he didn't belong here. The English working class didn't go on vacation to the medinas of Morocco, they went to cheap resorts in the south of Spain like Benidorm.

A red light went on in Grunt's head. Another went on when the guy didn't glance at him as one foreigner will usually do with another in such a place. Instead he took a casual interest in a stall selling the bright-yellow slippers that Moroccan men often wore.

Grunt wasn't fooled. Just because he couldn't see this guy watching him didn't mean he wasn't.

Grunt played it casual. He was lucky enough to already be walking on the opposite side of the street, so he continued to do so. He resisted the urge to move his hand closer to where the pistol he'd purchased from Ahmad was hidden under his loose shirt. He didn't want to advertise where he kept his weapon.

The street was narrow. It wouldn't take more than three or four steps for this guy to close with him. If he had a gun, he could shoot at point-blank range. Or was the stranger going to shadow him?

Grunt pulled out his phone and pretended to text someone. In fact he turned on his camera and put it on selfie mode.

He used it to take a quick glance over his shoulder.

The Englishman was still standing at the stall, holding a pair of slippers in his hands as the old man who ran it implored him to buy one. But the guy wasn't looking at the slippers.

He was looking right at Grunt.

CHAPTER 7

THIS IS GETTING BETTER *and better,* Grunt thought.

He walked as casually as he could down the street and turned the corner at the far end. Then he picked up speed and took a zigzag route through the alleys that ran through this neighborhood like a maze. He stopped once or twice at a corner to watch for pursuit, but none came.

Good. As usual, Grunt had scoped out the area, so he knew his way around. In a place like Marrakech, that was essential if you didn't want to get lost.

Or if you wanted to lose someone.

He took a roundabout route back to his hotel. There was a back way along a narrow alley, a small door opening into the kitchen. With luck, this guy hadn't found it yet.

He was in luck. No one was in the alley. He made his way to the door, pulled out his set of lock picks, and worked on the lock, hoping the deadbolt hadn't been put in place. Usually in Moroccan buildings, a door would only be bolted at night. In the daytime, the lock was considered enough because it was a pain to slide out the heavy bolt every time you wanted to use the door.

The lock opened with a click. He put away his tools and pushed on the door.

He was in luck again. It opened.

Grunt's nostrils were hit with the rich smell of a tagine cooking on the stove, and his ears were hit with a loud squawk from the hotel owner's wife, a heavyset woman in a voluminous djellaba. She seemed more angry than afraid that a foreigner had just picked the lock on her back door and walked in. Amid a stream of curses, she grabbed a skillet and raised it above her head.

Grunt looked her in the eye.

"I have a gun," he said in slow, careful Arabic. "But I'd like to save my bullets for someone other than you."

He'd stolen that line from a cheap Egyptian action flick, but it had the desired effect. She stepped back and lowered the skillet.

"My husband's a fool to let in foreigners like you. You're nothing but trouble. Get out of your room, you and your friend!"

Grunt paused. "My friend is in my room?"

"My husband let him in. I sure wouldn't have," the woman said, brandishing the skillet again. "Go find another place to stay, the both of you."

"Thank you. You've been very helpful."

He slipped past her, sped out of the kitchen before she decided to use the skillet, shoved the proprietor aside as he came to see who his wife was shouting at, and went to the stairs.

His room was just to the left of the upstairs landing, just out of sight. Grunt paused. Listened.

"Sir, my wife tells me—"

A quick glare over Grunt's shoulder silenced him. The man retreated to his kitchen, where his wife started scolding him in an angry whisper.

Grunt eased the pistol out from under his shirt and crept up the stairs. Luckily they were concrete, so his footsteps didn't make a sound.

He'd made it halfway up when a small noise from above made him pause.

Had that been the creak of a door hinge?

With infinite care, Grunt crept up the remaining stairs. The entire hotel seemed to have gone silent.

The woman he'd startled had stopped her shouting. The hotel proprietor wasn't speaking either. Grunt almost felt like going back down there and giving them some money to continue their argument. They knew something was up, and their silence was broadcasting that fact to whoever waited for him upstairs.

At the top of the stairs, Grunt got on his hands and knees. If the guy was around the corner aiming a gun, he'd have it at chest level. It would take a fraction of a second to adjust his aim.

A fraction of a second had saved Grunt's life before.

And it saved it now.

As he suspected, his door was open a crack. All he had time to see besides that was an eye and the muzzle of a gun behind that crack.

Grunt fired, then ducked back as the man returned fire, the bullet cracking off a chunk of concrete in the wall behind.

If Grunt had moved a fraction of a second later, his blood and brains would have been sprayed all over that wall.

Quick reactions and a good shot. That meant a professional.

Grunt stood at a crouch, whipped his hand around the corner long enough to fire a blind shot at the door, and hurried down the steps. He didn't think either of his two shots had gotten the guy. He just hoped the second one would delay him long enough that Grunt could find a better place to fight.

Suddenly the man he'd spotted outside appeared at the foot of the stairs. Not having time to raise his gun, Grunt leapt and hit him boots first. The man flew backward and landed hard on the floor with a thud.

Grunt whirled around, and as he suspected, the guy who had been waiting in his room already stood at the top of the stairs.

Grunt blinked. He was the exact duplicate of the man he'd just knocked down. Same features, same clothes, everything.

That split-second pause almost cost him his life.

There was a flash of metal, a red-hot pain along his wrist, and Grunt's pistol clattered to the floor.

Grunt ducked and went for his gun with his good hand and saw lying next to it what had injured him.

An old-fashioned straight razor.

A straight razor? Why hadn't the guy just shot him?

Just as Grunt was reaching for his gun, the man

on the floor kicked it away. The gun slid along the smooth tile floor a good ten feet.

Grunt booted the guy in the head then felt a slice of pain on his shoulder. The maniac on the stairs had thrown another straight razor. His twin on the floor, despite having just taken a kick to the head, was pulling one out of his pocket.

Who the hell uses straight razors as a weapon? Grunt wondered.

Maniacs, that's who. Grunt needed to end this fight now.

Grunt landed a kick to the guy's shoulder that should have dislocated it and sent the straight razor tumbling to the ground, but instead it only pushed him back a little. Then Grunt had to duck to the side to avoid another straight razor flying down the stairs at him.

Time to run.

Grunt bolted down the hall, making it around the corner just in time for another straight razor to miss him by inches. He entered the hotel's front lobby.

It was abandoned. This was another of those neighborhoods where people were good at detecting danger and made themselves scarce. Right next to the doorway Grunt had passed through stood a table with an ornate brass lamp. Grunt picked it up, spun around, and threw it into the face of one of the twins as he came around the corner. It landed with a satisfying thud, and the guy pirouetted back.

Losing no time, Grunt ran for the front door.

Only to find the other twin blocking it.

The guy must have jumped out of an upper window to get there so fast. These two were serious trouble.

Grunt ducked under a vicious swing with a straight razor and landed a fist in his opponent's stomach that would have doubled over a regular man. Instead it only brought out a little cough of air and made the guy take half a step back.

Grunt had to step back himself to avoid another swing of the razor, its keen blade gleaming in front of his eyes as it whooshed by.

Grunt grabbed his arm with both hands and twisted, bringing the man into an arm lock. His opponent responded by stomping on Grunt's foot and head-butting him.

"Two can play at that game," Grunt muttered and head-butted him back.

Before the fight could descend into a head-butting contest that he might not win, Grunt swept a leg under the guy's feet and dropped him on the floor.

Instinct told him to duck and turn.

Instinct saved his life for the moment.

A blade snicked by, scraping the top of his scalp. The other twin had recovered from getting twenty pounds of brass thrown in his face. These guys recovered remarkably quickly.

Grunt punched him then gasped as the maniac's razor cut a deep line down the side of his hip. Another slash across his chest made him stagger backward, almost tripping over the other man.

Then the twin in front of him thrust with his blade and took a deep gouge out of his gut.

That feels fatal, Grunt realized.

Once again, he ran.

He made it out the door and several yards down the street before the first of the razors flew after him and embedded itself in his shoulder blade. He made it another couple of yards before another slashed his calf and made him stumble. The crowd in the street screamed and parted, everyone heading for cover.

Jesus, how many razors do these guys have?

Just then he saw a sight that usually made him wary in this part of the world but at that moment felt as welcome as a Christmas tree surrounded by presents.

A policeman.

"Stop!" the man shouted in English, leveling his assault rifle to emphasize his point.

Grunt stumbled into the nearest alley. The cop, more interested in the identical twins throwing straight razors down the street, didn't follow.

Grunt didn't stick around to see the end of the story. He stumbled through the medina, passersby leaping out of his way. He came across a pharmacy, a little hole-in-the-wall place that sold bandages and aspirin to the local neighborhood. He lumbered in, threw some money at the startled woman behind the counter, and grabbed a bunch of cotton gauze, tape, iodine, and painkillers.

Next stop was a tailor's shop. In a narrow storefront no bigger than a closet, a man sat on a carpet with an old sewing machine, making and fixing clothing. He froze in terror as a huge Westerner, blood coursing out of half a dozen wounds and clutching a bag of medical equipment, relieved him of some needles and thread. He didn't even pick up the money the Westerner threw at him. It was soaked in blood.

Grunt found the dead end of an alley to hide in,

swallowed a bunch of painkillers, and got to work on his wounds. He didn't have time to wait for the painkillers to kick in, not with all this bleeding. Wiping iodine on his hands and on the wounds to clean them as much as possible, he used the needle and thread to sew up the cuts and then covered them with cotton gauze and tape. The pain kept his mind sharp. A good thing, because he already felt a bit dizzy from blood loss. The stitches and bandages would stop the bleeding, but the deep cut to his gut must be bleeding internally. There was no way for him to stop that himself, and he didn't dare go to a hospital. He'd be arrested for sure.

And he didn't have anyone he could ask for help. Ahmad Chukri was clear on the other side of town, and Grunt didn't have his phone number. He wasn't the kind of person to give it out. Not a chance that he could get there undetected, assuming he could even get there at all.

So he was left with one option—hiding out here and hoping his body could stop its own internal bleeding and survive the injuries.

Twelve hours later, in the dark of the night, Grunt had to admit to himself that that was not going to happen. He could feel himself weakening with every hour. The painkillers gave him a pleasant fuzzy feeling, the only sensation coming from his various cuts being a bit of tightness. But he could sense the life ebbing out of him. He was a goner.

Damn. He didn't want to end like this. Otto needed him. Jaxon needed him. The others could take care of themselves, but the kids needed him alive.

So the only option is to live, soldier.

Grunt shifted his weight again, bending one leg to get it beneath him. Then he tried to rise.

He fell before he got halfway up, pain jabbing through the medicinal fog. He gritted his teeth and tried again.

In the pitch darkness of a forgotten alley, unseen by anyone, Grunt started the toughest struggle of his life.

CHAPTER 8

AUGUST 14, 2016, THE ROAD BETWEEN
TIMBUKTU AND RAS EL MA
4:30 P.M.

Jaxon was startled at how quickly they passed through the green zone around the River Niger. Within a few minutes, they had left the cultivated farmland behind. The last little irrigation channel ended, and the desert took over. Then for hours nothing lay on either side of the dusty, narrow highway except rolling dunes and a few dried-up little shrubs. Civilization clustered around water in this part of the world, and water was scarce.

They headed west, along the shores of what the map called Lake Faguibine. There was no lake. Jaxon guessed that in the rainy season, there might be a lake or something that kind of looked like a lake, but all she saw out the passenger's-side window was a valley surrounded by gray, shelving rock with a few palm trees and bushes at the bottom. She spotted the occasional flock of sheep or goats and figured there must be some water down there somewhere. But a lake? She hadn't seen a lake in a long, long time.

She was amazed every time they passed a little village. How could anyone live here? She supposed they didn't have any choice. The better land by the river was all taken, and these people didn't have the money to go anywhere else.

And to think her people were fleeing neighboring Mauritania to come here for a better life! The worst of it all was that Mali probably would give them a better life. At least they wouldn't be persecuted.

What was going on? Why was the Mauritanian government hunting down the Atlanteans? General Meade couldn't be directing all this, not all the way over here. Besides, he had plenty of Atlanteans to mess with back in the States. So was someone else looking to enslave her people?

Why couldn't everyone just leave her alone? All her life, she'd been picked on for being different. She had never fit in, and now that she had found her place in the world, she discovered that she was a member of a people who had been suffering persecution for centuries.

"Just my luck," she muttered.

"Sorry?" Salif Amar asked from the back seat. He'd come along to act as translator. Vivian, sitting behind the wheel, didn't even glance at Jaxon when she had talked to herself. She'd gotten used to Jaxon's habits long ago.

"Nothing," Jaxon grumbled. "I'm just mad at all the crap our people have to put up with."

Salif shrugged. "Yes, sometimes we have trouble, but we have a great history, and each of us has something special about us."

"What do you mean?" Jaxon asked, turning in her seat.

Salif looked confused. "You know."

Jaxon felt confused for a moment. "Oh, you mean how we're stronger and faster than other people?"

"We don't really talk about that around outsiders," Salif chided, glancing nervously at Vivian.

"Does everyone have special powers too? I can make plants grow. Can you do that, or is your power different?"

Salif stared at her like she'd just shouted her most intimate details in the middle of a crowded theater.

"H-how can you say that in front of just anybody?" he finally spit out.

"Anybody? Vivian's not 'anybody.' She saved my life."

Salif glared at her. "We don't talk about these things with outsiders."

Vivian caught his eye in the rearview mirror. "I'm on your side, honey."

Salif clicked his tongue. "We've heard that many times before."

He crossed his arms, looked out the window, and said no more. They drove in awkward silence for the rest of the way.

The village of Ras el Ma looked even worse than Jaxon had imagined it. It stood on the edge of the "lake," a sad collection of adobe huts and a few ugly concrete buildings. They didn't get to see any more of it because a police checkpoint stopped them at the edge of town. A pair of cops with Kalashnikovs studied the two Land Rovers curiously.

Salif stepped out and spoke with them.

"What are they saying?" Jaxon whispered to Vivian.

"My Arabic isn't too good, honey, but I think they're wondering why we don't have the Doctors Without Borders logo on our vehicles. Sounds like they've set up a refugee camp on the other side of town."

Jaxon nodded. She'd heard of the organization. They went to all the troubled areas of the world and provided medical care. At least someone did something for her people.

The conversation continued for several minutes, with Jaxon growing more and more anxious. The last time they'd had to deal with cops, they'd been shot at. Of course, that had been in Mauritania. Mali seemed more chilled out. She still hadn't gotten used to policemen toting assault rifles, though. She also didn't like how the younger cop kept peeking in the window and leering at her and Vivian.

At last Salif climbed back into the Land Rover.

"They'll let us pass. I told them I am looking for family members. That is true in a way."

They passed through the little village, maneuvering around a group of chickens pecking at something on the dirt road that passed for a main street in this place. Jaxon wondered if the chickens were eating seeds dropped from some truck. Back in Mauritania, she had made a bunch of them grow into vines that had trapped a cop who had tried to arrest them. She smiled at the memory. If every one of her people had powers like that, the world better start treating them better! She'd have to talk about it with Salif once he stopped pouting.

After a minute, they left the village and sped out onto a flat stretch of barren desert.

Jaxon caught her breath. Before them, a huge tent village stretched across the sand. Dozens of bright-white tents stood in the sunlight, and beyond those stood smaller tents made of tarpaulins, old blankets, plastic sheets, or whatever else the refugees could find to shelter themselves from the Saharan sun.

A small painted wooden sign in front read, "*Médecins Sans Frontières. Camp de réfugiés Ras el Ma.*" Below that were several words written in Arabic, presumably saying the same thing.

Just behind the sign stood a large tent with open sides. Inside was a row of examination tables and smaller tables beside them covered with medical equipment. Several doctors treated a large crowd of patients, mostly women holding small children and babies.

Jaxon felt her mouth go dry and her heart start beating faster. Vivian parked the Land Rover next to a couple of trucks bearing the Doctors Without Borders logo. Dr. Yamazaki parked the other Land Rover next to them.

Jaxon stepped out into the sunlight, but even in the 110-degree heat, she felt a chill. There must be thousands of people here. The rows of tents seemed to stretch forever. People began to gather to stare at the newcomers, as they did in every little town or village they'd stopped in as they crossed the Sahara.

This time it was different.

Everyone was thin to the point of emaciation. Sunken eyes in skull-like faces fixed on them. The people—the elderly, the women, and especially the children—all had a lost, exhausted look to them. She saw very few men and wondered what had happened to them.

Jaxon scanned the crowd for people with Atlantean features but didn't see anyone.

A man in a doctor's coat came through the crowd. He was black but obviously not from here. He looked too well fed. Even the healthy people in places like Mauritania and Mali tended to look too thin, with sharp features and skin battered by a lifetime spent in the punishing sun, but not this man. He looked like he was in his early forties and had lived a healthy life.

"*Bonjour,*" he said, then asked a question in French.

"Um, do you speak English?" Jaxon asked, feeling foolish.

"Yes. You're not the delivery of rehydration packs, are you?" he said in English with a French accent.

"No, sorry."

"Then what are you bringing?" he asked in a tone that told her that he didn't have time to waste. Now that Jaxon got a closer look at him, she could see his eyes were red and puffy from lack of sleep.

Jaxon decided not to waste this guy's time. If he was running this place, every minute counted.

"I'm staying in Timbuktu. I'm American, but I'm one of the People of the Sea."

The man's brow furrowed. "What's that?"

"An ethnic group in this region. Did you just fly in?"

"Usually I work south of the Sahara. My last postings were the Congo and Burundi. My team and I came last month when the government asked us in to help with the crisis, and I haven't had time for sightseeing," the man said with a dismissive wave of the hand. It was obvious he had already tired of the conversation. He glanced back at the tent, where his colleagues were busy giving medical aid to the refugees.

Jaxon cut to the chase.

"My people are being persecuted in Mauritania, and my community in Timbuktu has decided to shelter any of the People of the Sea we find here. We came because we saw a photo of one family in the newspaper."

The doctor looked away from her to Vivian and Dr. Yamazaki before resting his eyes on Salif.

"Are you one of these Sea People too?" the doctor asked him.

"Yes."

"How many housing units do you have?"

"Several dozen homes."

"That may not be enough."

Jaxon cut in. "If it isn't, we have the money to put them up at one of the hotels."

The doctor glanced at Jaxon and turned back to Salif. The conversation continued without her. She wondered if she was being dismissed because she was a teenager or because she was a girl. Perhaps both.

"Do you have the money to feed them?" the doctor asked.

"Yes."

"What about medical care?"

Dr. Yamazaki said, "There's a physician in their community, plus my colleague and I are both geneticists and trained in basic medical practices."

"They don't need genetic work, they need rehydration packets, a good diet, and proper shelter. A lot of the children are suffering from diarrhea, and everyone suffered a shortage of water getting here."

"They will get all these," Salif said.

"I know how to mix rehydration packets to UNICEF standards," Dr. Yamazaki said. "I was mixing some up just yesterday. A member of our team got a bad case of food poisoning."

"What's the recipe?" the doctor asked as if Dr. Yamazaki was a medical student.

"Eight teaspoons of sugar and one of salt per liter of water. I also put in a bit of lemon juice for the electrolytes and vitamin C. I'd add mashed bananas for the potassium if I could find some."

"Good enough," the doctor nodded. "Did you bring any with you?"

"Eighty liters, a little over twenty gallons."

"Give it to me."

It came out as an order, not a request. Jaxon couldn't believe this guy's rudeness.

Dr. Yamazaki shrugged and went off to the Land Rover. A minute later, she brought back two large plastic jugs, which the doctor took from her.

"Can we go through the camp and search for my people?" Jaxon asked. She was sick of being passed over in this conversation.

The doctor sized her up for a moment before replying. "Well, I can't stop you. Any burden off my back is welcome. You better clear it with the local authorities, though. I don't think they want the refugees wandering around the countryside."

Without another word, he turned and went back to the medical tent. He immediately moved to an examination table. A long line of patients stood before it. The first in line was a woman carrying a tiny baby. With expert care, the doctor put it on a scale and started taking notes. Then he gave the infant an injection.

Jaxon's attitude toward this brusque man softened. This was what they'd been keeping him from. She could forgive him for being curt.

"Well, let's get this done," Jaxon said with a sigh.

They walked down one of the rows of tents. The tents nearer the medical station bore the Doctors Without Borders logo and were made of new canvas. Inside each, they saw a dozen or more people, most lying on new blankets that had obviously been issued by the charity. They lay as still as statues, utterly worn out from their ordeal. Jaxon peered at each face, looking for the features of her people. The refugees peered back, some curious, others hopeful, but most without any expression at all.

"These people have been through too much," Salif said, shaking his head sadly. "With all the rebel groups in Mauritania, no place is safe. The rebels will come into a village and demand food and money at gunpoint. Then the government soldiers come and punish the villagers for helping the rebels."

They continued. Although the camp was clean, it stank of unwashed bodies and the smell of sickness. There was little conversation, the only sounds being coughs and sighs and the wailing of infants. A small crowd of the healthier adults had gathered to follow them.

"Ask them if they've seen any of our people around," Jaxon told Salif. She found herself whispering. This place creeped her out.

Salif talked to them for a minute. One older man,

clutching a naked toddler at his side, replied and pointed further into the camp.

Jaxon looked where he indicated, and her heart fell. Doctors Without Borders obviously hadn't brought enough tents, because beyond the tidy rows of their shelters sprawled a chaotic mass of tents and lean-tos made of any material the refugees could scrounge. She'd seen this section of the camp coming in, but now that she was closer, it looked even worse. No wonder the doctor had immediately asked what they were bringing. Their team was stuck in the middle of nowhere. Any supplies must take ages to get here, and they hadn't arrived with enough. Now they had to wait for more.

It didn't look like some of these people could wait very long.

The old man led them along. He looked of Arab descent, with olive skin and lean features made leaner through malnutrition. He talked amiably to Salif in Arabic.

"This man says he lived in a village in the central part of Mauritania and had many of our people as neighbors. The village healer was one of the People of the Sea. It sounds like we had a good reputation there."

"Ask him what happened."

Salif talked with him a minute as the man hobbled down the sandy lane. Now that there was a conversation people could understand, more had gathered around. As the old man spoke, several others cut in to add something. After a minute, Salif translated.

"All of these people tell the same story. The police and army came to their villages or farms looking for our people, saying the People of the Sea were enemies of the state and trying to overthrow the government and take power for themselves. Since our people have a good reputation, most Arabs and Tuaregs did not believe them. So the authorities told them that anyone who sheltered us would be arrested too. Some of our people managed to run away or hide. The rest were taken."

Jaxon felt a cold knot in the pit of her stomach.

Vivian asked the question Jaxon was afraid to ask. "Where were they taken?"

"They do not know," Salif said. "Perhaps our people will."

CHAPTER 9

THEY HAD ENTERED the shabbier part of the camp and passed along narrow paths between tents made with blankets or plastic sheeting. Even so, the place looked clean and organized. A circle of women cooked bread on a piece of sheet metal placed on a small fire. A group of younger women dug a latrine off to one side. Others cared for children or fanned old people who lay prostrate in the heat. Anyone who had the energy to work was working. While the arrival of Doctors Without Borders was certainly a blessing, these people were helping themselves too.

Suddenly Jaxon stopped in her tracks. One large tent, made of several bedsheets sewn together, was open at the front. Inside she saw several of her people.

She counted about twenty of them, all women

and children except for one old man who looked half dead. When they saw Jaxon and Salif, they looked up in surprise. Some of the women and children rose. The others, too weak to move, sat and stared.

Salif exchanged words with several of them in Arabic. The women started wailing, and Salif began to cry too. Jaxon's own eyes began to tear up even though she didn't know what they were saying. The looks on their faces said enough.

Several women came over and embraced Jaxon. They touched her Western clothing and asked her questions.

"Salif, tell them about me, and tell them we're going to take them to safety in Timbuktu."

He did, and after another minute of conversation, they were invited into the tent to sit down. Remarkably, one of the women pulled out a nearly empty tin of tea, pulled out the last leaves from the bottom, and put them in a kettle on top of a campfire near the entrance to the tent.

"They're going to serve us tea?" Jaxon said, amazed.

Salif smiled. "We are in their home."

"We can't drink the last of their tea!"

"It would be rude to refuse their hospitality,

honey," Vivian said. "That's how people are here. It's one of the reasons I love this part of the world."

As cups of tea got passed around, the Atlantean refugees told their story. Salif translated.

"I'm afraid they do not know much more than the villagers we spoke to before. It came suddenly. There was no announcement from the government. Armed officers from either the police or the army showed up at each village and town and announced that our people were traitors. There was no time to prepare. It had all been done in secret and timed to happen all at once all over the country. Not even the local government people knew of this until they were given their orders the day before. The only ones who escaped were those who had friends in the armed forces who warned them that night. Even so, as you can see, they didn't have time to leave with anything more than the clothes they wore and a few essentials. They have been walking through the desert for days. Some have died along the way."

Jaxon bit her lip.

"How many are in this camp?" she asked.

"Just those you see here and another small tent," Salif said.

"It's going to be a tight squeeze, but we can probably get them all in the two Land Rovers," Vivian said. "It's better to take them all now while we can. We don't want to give those policemen time to change their minds."

"Do they have any idea where the others were taken?" Dr. Yamazaki asked.

Salif shook his head. "Only rumors. One sympathetic police officer said they were all to be taken to a camp just north of Tidjikja. That is in the center of the country. It is a lonely place. There is desert all around."

"A camp," Jaxon said, trembling. "Like a concentration camp?"

Salif's usually smiling face darkened. "Perhaps, yes."

"We need to get them out of here," Jaxon said. "Are they willing to come?"

"I have already asked. Yes, they will."

"But why didn't they fight back?" Jaxon asked, suddenly angry. "They're stronger and faster and have powers they could have used."

Salif's face hardened. "We should go."

Dr. Yamazaki pulled out her medical bag.

"Before we go, I'll give them each a quick medical examination. Vivian, can you help? I'm sure you have some field medical training. Salif, will you translate?"

"Of course. One moment, please."

Salif took Jaxon aside. "Remember what I told you in the Land Rover?"

"About not revealing our powers to outsiders? Yeah, what's up with that?"

"It is dangerous to be different."

Jaxon bit her lip. She knew a bit about that, and she was beginning to understand a whole lot more. Salif went on.

"When people see you as different, it is easy for bad people to say you are the enemy. This has happened before in other places with other peoples. You must remember that this is a dangerous region. The governments here rule by fear and force. With so many bandits and Islamic militias, I suppose they have to, but to keep their power, they know it is best to make an enemy who everyone can blame for their problems. Sadly, right now they are using us."

"But why? We never harmed anyone."

"No, but we are different and always have been. We have a reputation as sorcerers. Even though we hide our abilities, people whisper of them. They know we can do things no normal man or woman could, and while some look at us as blessed healers like that old Arab man who led us here, others think we have made a pact with the Devil."

"That's silly."

"There is no good magic in Islam. Only the Devil works magic. If they see a human being doing something that looks like magic, many people will think that person is in league with dark forces."

"But we've never hurt anybody. Why should they fear us?"

Salif shook his head sadly. "Have you forgotten your history? Atlantis fell because we lost the way. We began to fight one another, and we began to be arrogant and violent to other peoples as well. The Arabs and the Europeans and the Black Africans may have forgotten the stories we preserve, but they have remembered that those who do what seems to be magic are to be feared. Our griot told me this. It was one of his most important lessons."

Jaxon blinked. She didn't know much about history, but she did know that witches had been burned in the past because the authorities thought they cast spells. Even some early scientists had been attacked for doing what seemed to be impossible. People got thrown in jail for saying the Earth revolved around the sun. One night on the trip across the Sahara, Dr. Yuhle had told them a story about how the first people to fly a balloon in France back in the eighteenth century had landed near a village, and the villagers had attacked the balloon with pitchforks, thinking it was a monster. The scientists had barely escaped with their lives.

So was all that some sort of race memory from a time when Atlanteans, with all their superior powers and special abilities, had lorded it over the rest of the world? Were they really feared because of the sins of the past?

Jaxon sat and watched Dr. Yamazaki give each Atlantean a medical exam. She felt a bit useless. She couldn't talk to her people and couldn't help them with their dehydration or illnesses. At least she could get them out of here.

The exams took a couple of hours, and during all that time, only one member of Doctors Without Borders came to see what was going on. A nurse popped her head in the tent, had a quick technical conversation with Dr. Yamazaki, and hurried off. With thousands of people to take care of, the organization left the Atlantis Allegiance to do their thing.

Once she was finished, Dr. Yamazaki sat down for another cup of tea.

"So there are twenty-seven Atlanteans in all, almost all women and children as you can see. Most are suffering from dehydration and exhaustion and borderline malnutrition. Other than that, there are a few cholera cases, some eye infections, and one older woman with a serious heart condition. I can treat the cholera and the infections, but there's nothing I can do for the heart case. She has a couple of months at most. There's also someone I suspect has cancer of the liver. There's nothing I can do about that either."

Jaxon was shocked at how detached the scientist sounded while talking about these people, her people. Then she realized that, like the rude French doctor they'd spoken to when they arrived, that sort of detachment was probably the only way to stay sane in a job like this.

"Perhaps we can do something back in Timbuktu for those two cases," Vivian said without much hope in her voice. "It's getting late, and we're going to need to get going. I don't want to drive through the dark."

"But there are 27 of them. How are they all going to fit?"

Salif chuckled. "Haven't you seen our public buses? They can ride on the roof and cling to the sides."

"All the way?" Jaxon gaped.

The Atlantean shrugged. "It's better than staying here."

It took only a few minutes for the Atlantean

refugees to gather their meager possessions and head to the Land Rovers.

There they found the two policemen from the checkpoint waiting for them.

"Hello, where going?" the older one said in bad English. The younger one stood next to Jaxon, too close. He gave her a smile, and she glowered back at him.

Salif said something in Arabic, and the older guard snapped an angry reply. Salif pleaded, sounding conciliatory, but the man only clicked his tongue in disgust and rubbed his thumb and forefinger together.

Salif turned to Jaxon. "He wants a bribe."

"What? That's illegal!" Jaxon spun on the older guard and jabbed a finger in his chest. "Wait until the head of Doctors Without Borders hears about this."

Jaxon stormed off toward the medical tent.

"No, wait!" Vivian called after her. Jaxon ignored her. She'd had enough of this. Her people were suffering out here in the desert, and all the local cops could do was ask for bribes?

Shouldering her way past a couple of nurses, she found the head doctor bent over an examination table setting a broken leg.

"The guards are demanding a bribe to let us leave," Jaxon told him.

"Pay it then," the doctor muttered as he coated the leg with plaster.

"What?"

"I said pay it. Otherwise they won't let you go," he replied, adjusting his position so he could put some more plaster on a different part of the leg. He didn't even look at Jaxon.

"But it's illegal!"

"So's genocide. And that's what you're trying to save your people from. That's what you said, isn't it? So pay the damn bribe and stop bothering me."

"What's your problem, anyway?"

The doctor stood up straight and looked at her for the first time.

"If you don't pay the bribe, they won't let you go. Then they'll cause trouble for me and my team. I have a few thousand people to take care of here. You want to interfere with that just because you don't want to spend any of Daddy's money?"

Jaxon snarled. "Daddy's money? It's not Daddy's money. You don't know a thing about me!"

"I know you have no idea what you're doing. You still think you're in some suburban shopping mall. Damn Americans think their money can get them anything they want. Well, use your money to buy your way out of the trouble you got yourself into and leave me alone. I'm busy."

The doctor bent over his work again. Jaxon sputtered, trying to form words. After a moment, she threw her hands in the air and stormed out of the tent.

"How did that go, honey?" Vivian asked when she returned. The two cops were still there. The Atlanteans had sat down, looking glum and resigned. Jaxon realized they thought they weren't going to get to leave.

"He said to pay the bribe."

"We have to, honey. Otherwise they'll give him trouble."

"He said that too."

Jaxon shook her head, feeling foolish. Daouda Ndiaye's words came back to her.

Don't make the same mistake many Americans make, thinking that money can solve all life's problems. Some problems can't be solved with money but only with wisdom and cooperation.

Jaxon sighed. She realized that as annoying as the doctor was, she had once again judged him too harshly. He had a hard job to do, and her being stubborn would only make it harder.

"How much do they want?" she asked Salif.

This led to a long haggle in Arabic before Salif turned back to her. "Two hundred dollars, in dollars. They want hard currency. It's better than the West African franc, which is worth less and less each month."

Jaxon sighed and pulled out her money belt, a special belt with a zipper pouch that went under her shirt. Vivian had given it to her, saying it was a good way to stop pickpockets. As she did so, Vivian moved to get between her and the cops. Jaxon realized this was to keep them from seeing how much money she had. Asking for two hundred bucks was taking most of the money she had on her, but not all. If they saw more, they'd probably ask for more.

She handed over the money, and the guards walked off, chuckling.

The Atlantis Allegiance crammed everyone into the Land Rovers. Every adult had a child or two sitting on their lap, and the younger, healthier people sat on the roof or stood on the running board and gripped the roof rack.

Soon they set out into the desert, the laughing cops waving them goodbye. The Land Rovers moved slowly to keep the people on top of the vehicles from falling off. Once they got out of sight of the refugee camp, Jaxon felt better. She never wanted to see a place like that again.

She looked around at her fellow Atlanteans. None of them seemed happy or grateful to be on their way. In fact, a couple of them started crying. One old woman looked longingly out the back window.

"What's the matter?" she asked Salif in a whisper.

"They are sad to be going further from their homes. They are leaving their husbands and sons behind."

Jaxon bit her lip. She had been expecting a joyful ride home, with everyone singing and clapping. Now she realized what a silly dream that had been. She'd been expecting to buy their happiness and make herself happy by doing so. Once again the griot's words came back to her.

Some problems can't be solved with money but only with wisdom and cooperation.

Where was she going to find the wisdom to protect her people from so many enemies?

CHAPTER 10

AUGUST 14, 2016, HOTEL CARAVANE,
TIMBUKTU, MALI
8:00 P.M.

Otto was worried, and he was bored.

Mostly he was worried.

He'd been left behind again as most of the Atlantis Allegiance had driven west to pick up the Atlantean refugees. That meant another boring day stuck alone in his hotel room. Dr. Yuhle dropped in every now and then to see how he was doing but spent most of the time in the manuscript museum. He was excited about some discovery he'd made but didn't have time to explain it to Otto. Otto was left with nothing to do and no one to do it with.

He found himself wishing Nadya would come back.

Unfortunately, the lovely Russian woman hadn't given him her phone number or said where she was staying. She was probably off doing another of her photography projects.

Everyone got to do something cool except him.

Otto looked at his watch. Eight o'clock in the evening already? The people who had gone to the refugee camp should have been back by now. In fact, they should have been back two hours ago. He wondered if they were having some trouble. He'd tried calling an hour ago, but they hadn't picked up. That meant they couldn't get a signal, a common problem in this part of the world. Or it might mean they couldn't answer for some reason.

He didn't want to think about that second possibility.

He dialed Jaxon's number again. Still no answer. He tried Vivian's and Dr. Yamazaki's. Same result.

"Why the hell am I even here?" he asked the four walls of his hotel room. They didn't answer either.

At least he was feeling a bit better. Not enough

to risk a walk across town to the manuscript museum or to go sightseeing, but at least enough to go to the nearest market and get some matches.

So he sat on the end of his bed playing one of his favorite games, one his cousin had taught him when they were kids. He took a box of wooden matches and removed one. Setting the tip of the match against the black striking strip of the matchbox and pressing down on the end with his forefinger to hold it in place, he flicked it with his middle finger. The match hissed to life and sailed across the room like a little meteor. It landed and extinguished itself on the concrete floor.

Otto smiled. This game always made him feel better.

He took out another match and sent it after the previous one. He'd drawn faint circles on the floor with a pencil and assigned them points. Ten points for the closest and biggest circle, twenty-five for one further away, and a hundred for a little one against the far wall. That one was tricky. He'd tried bouncing the matches off the wall, but they always bounced too far and missed the target. He found that he had to arc them just right to make them land inside. No points if they hit the circle but went out.

His last box of matches had won him 245 points, down from his previous score of 330. So far, this matchbox looked like it was going for the record. He already had two matches in the hundred-point circle and three more in the twenty-five-point circle, and only a few misses. He tried not to think of the mess he was making or whether the little burn marks would wash off the walls and floor.

At least he was being cautious and had moved all the flammable stuff out of that side of the room. It made the game less fun because there wasn't any risk, but he didn't want anyone shouting at him.

Just as he was flicking his next match, a knock at the door made him leap up. The burning match fell on his bed.

He slapped it out, cursing under his breath as he burned his hand.

The knock came again.

"Coming!" he called, hoping whoever it was spoke English.

He went to the door and opened it a crack.

Nadya stood in the hallway, her bulky camera bag slung over one shoulder.

"Oh, hi!" he said, feeling flustered. Damn, she was good looking.

"Are you feeling better? Dimitri is still at the

museum with your friend, and I am bored." She sniffed and looked past him. "Is something burning?"

Before Otto could object, she pushed her way into the room. Otto tensed when he felt the warmth of her body pressing by him.

She looked at the mess on the floor and chuckled.

"Oh dear, someone else is bored too."

"Um, well, it's…"

"Ah, it's a game!" she said, pointing at one of the circles. "You have to get the matches in the circles, yes? The numbers written by them are points."

Otto gave her a sheepish smile. "Yeah. I was bored, like you said."

"So where do you fire from, the bed?" she put her camera bag down and sat on the end of the bed.

She patted the space next to her. "Show me this game, and then I'll teach you one from my country."

Otto gulped and closed the door.

"Lock it," Nadya said, "We wouldn't want the hotel staff interrupting us, would we?"

"Um, no. No, we wouldn't," he replied, doing as she asked.

Otto sat down next to her on the bed, putting as much space between them as possible. Nadya closed the gap and said, "So, teach me this game."

Otto gulped again and pulled out a box of

matches. "Well, you fire them like this, see?" He shot a match. It flared up and traced a fiery arc across the room to land in the twenty-five-point circle. "Each of us gets a full box of matches and fires them all. Whoever gets the most points wins. Yeah, I know, it's kinda dumb."

Nadya shrugged. "You are stuck alone in a hotel room with no television and no internet access. What else are you going to do? It's more fun than I have with Dimitri."

The mention of Nadya's companion made him suddenly nervous. "Shouldn't they be back by now?"

She shook her head, annoyed. "No, he and your friend Yuhle said they would stay late and then get some dinner in town. They are celebrating some big discovery they made. I do not know what, and I do not care. Of course they did not invite me. That is fine, because they will only talk about dusty old manuscripts and old dead ruins. I like living things."

Nadya fixed him with a steady gaze. A little smile stole around the corners of her lips.

She took a match out of the box, set it into position, and flicked it. The hiss of the flame made Otto feel all tingly. Something about the combination of fire and a beautiful woman was intoxicating.

You already have a girlfriend, he reminded

himself. *And Nadya is ten years older than you. Plus she's way out of your league.*

"Ah! I got twenty-five points!" she said. "Let's see if you can do better."

"Beginner's luck. You can't beat an old pro like me."

Otto fired, and his flaming match landed in the twenty-five-point circle, knocking Nadya's match out of it.

Nadya nudged him. She moved up to sit right next to him, her leg pressed against his. "Oh, you like to play rough, eh? Do I lose my points?"

"Oh no, I'm a perfect gentleman. Knocking the other person's match out of the circle only counts as bragging rights."

Nadya nudged him again and winked.

"Well, let's see if we can give you more to brag about, eh?"

That can't mean what I think it means.

Nadya's next shot earned her another twenty-five points. Otto's hands shook so much he couldn't even light his match.

"So where is everybody?" Nadya asked.

"Out of town. They went to see some refugees near the border."

"And they left you all alone? Bah! They treat you

the way Dimitri treats me. We are orphans together in Timbuktu, yes?"

"I suppose so."

"When will they come back?"

Otto shrugged. "They haven't called me. I hope they're all right."

"I am sure they are fine. You know how bad the signal is here. If they aren't in a town, there is no hope of calling."

"Yeah, they said they'd call when they reached the outskirts of Timbuktu."

"Oh, I see. And it only takes about twenty minutes to get to the hotel from the highway. That gives us twenty minutes' warning."

Otto turned to her. "Warning? Warning for what?"

Nadya smiled at him again. He wished Jaxon smiled at him like that more often. Jaxon was so preoccupied all the time. Apparently this Dimitri guy, who he'd only met once briefly, acted the same way.

"We will have twenty minutes to get cleaned up," she said.

"Um, what?"

This really can't be happening.

Nadya spread out a hand to encompass all the matches spread around the floor.

"To clean up your room."

"Oh yeah, right."

Otto wasn't convinced that was really what she meant. Something in her tone and her mischievous look told him so.

That's just your imagination. Besides, you've got a girlfriend, dummy. Stop fantasizing about other women.

But was it really just a fantasy? The way the side of her body remained pressed against his sure wasn't a fantasy. Women didn't just do that by accident.

They kept flicking matches. The score remained close until Otto landed one in the hundred-point circle.

"You are too good at this!" Nadya said. "But I am good at other things. You will see."

This can't be happening.

Otto tried to edge away, but there was no room left on the narrow bed. If he edged away any more, he'd end up on the floor.

"So do you all stay in this hall?" Nadya asked, turning to him. Their faces were close, and Otto could feel the warmth of her breath.

"Yeah, we got rooms all together. We basically

took over this wing of the hotel," Otto replied, thinking it was an odd question.

"So you and your girlfriend don't get any privacy. Why doesn't she stay here with you?"

Otto looked away, flustered. "Well, we're not really, um..."

"You're not really boyfriend and girlfriend?"

Don't you dare lie, Otto told himself.

"Well, um, we are. It's just that's she's not, you know, ready."

Nadya put a hand on his cheek. "Poor boy. You are such a handsome young man. You deserve better treatment."

Otto froze. This woman was definitely coming on to him.

He fumbled for his phone.

"I better check in on them. They said they'd be back by now."

He called Jaxon and listened to it ring. Nadya reclined on the bed and watched him. He tried not to look at her. Tried and failed. She was gorgeous. Jaxon's phone rang at least ten times before he finally gave up.

Next he tried to call Vivian, then Dr. Yamazaki. No luck.

"I don't understand why they aren't picking up,"

Otto muttered.

Nadya plucked the phone from his hand and set it aside. "Of course you do. You said it yourself. They are away from a signal. And they told you they would call once they picked up the signal from here in town. As soon as they get off the highway, they will call you, so why worry? Come, talk to me. I have been bored all day."

Nadya tugged at him until he was lying on the bed next to her. His heart pounded so hard in his chest he swore she must be able to hear it.

"Don't look so nervous, Otto! I won't bite. Tell me more about your girlfriend. How did you meet?"

"We, um, went to school together." He didn't want to mention that they were in a group home together. People got judgmental about that sort of stuff, and he definitely wanted Nadya to have a good impression of him.

"Is she good at school?"

"She didn't really care about the subjects, to be honest. Plus she's dyslexic."

"That is too bad. I bet you are smart."

"I did get As most of the time." *Not that my parents cared.*

"I knew it! I could tell you were intelligent the

first moment I saw you. So how did you end up in Timbuktu, and where are your parents?"

"Jaxon doesn't actually know her parents, I mean..." At the last moment, Otto remembered the cover story they were traveling under. "Vivian's her mom, but she doesn't know her dad. Grunt's my dad." That felt kind of good to say, he realized. "He and my mom split up."

"So you came to Timbuktu to research Jaxon's father, maybe find him?"

"Um, something like that." He didn't like the way these questions were headed. He didn't want to lie to Nadya, but he couldn't tell her the truth.

"Did you like the trip here? You drove, correct?"

Otto realized that he had already let slip at their last meeting that they had driven across the Sahara. That looked suspicious, because no sane person would drive through Mauritania, especially not in the middle of summer. Only someone with something to hide would do that, which of course they did.

He had to be careful. Nadya was friendly, a bit too friendly, but he shouldn't let out too much information to anyone.

"Yeah, well, we drove from the coast and up

through the desert. We didn't go into any other countries."

As soon as he said it, he realized how obvious and stupid a lie it sounded. Nadya didn't seem to notice at all.

"Oh, that is right. You told me your father is an archaeologist."

"Um, yeah. We were looking for ancient ruins in the desert."

Nadya leaned closer. "Did you find anything interesting?"

"I thought you weren't interested in dusty old ruins."

"I'm interested in anything you do."

Otto chuckled, both from nerves and from the silliness of it all. Here he was lying on a bed with a gorgeous Russian woman ten years older than he was, and she said that kind of thing. His friends back home would never believe him.

Home? Friends? What counted as home, anyway? Certainly not his parents' house. The group home? Not that either. And what friends? Sure, he had always been popular, but he'd been shuffled around among so many schools and group homes that none of those friends ever lasted. He had a couple of hundred friends on Twitter, all people who would love to hang out with him if he wasn't on the other side of the world, but he couldn't even remember all their faces.

"Why did you laugh?" Nadya asked. She ran a finger along the line of his jaw. "You laughed and then got all serious."

Otto sat up. This was going too far. "Look, Nadya. Thanks for coming and all, but I'm still not a hundred percent, you know? I should rest."

Nadya remained lying on the bed. "Rest? Nonsense! You've been resting all day."

"Yeah, but I'm kind of tired."

Nadya got up on one elbow, looking hurt. "You are not tired. What is the matter? Are you shy?"

"No, it's just that, well, if Jaxon came in, she might get the wrong idea."

Nadya laughed. Otto blushed, thinking she was laughing at him.

"Who is to say it is the wrong idea? Oh now, don't get that face. I am sorry if I am too forward. It is just that you are so handsome, and I am very lonely here. It happens when you go to the far places of the world. This is your first time out of your country, yes? You will see what I mean."

She sat up. Otto was relieved to see she left some space between them.

"So tell me about these archaeological sites your father was looking at. Were the cave paintings very beautiful?"

"How did you know we found cave paintings?"

Nadya's eyes sparked. "Oh, so you did! There are many out in the desert, next to ancient towns. I like to photograph them. Do you have any photos of them?"

"I'd love to show them to you, but I don't have any. They're on another computer."

Nadya studied him. "Whose computer?"

"Why does that matter?"

"Oh, nothing, I was just curious. Here, I brought you something. I hope they are still cold."

She unzipped her bag and pulled out two bottles of beer. He raised his eyebrows. He hadn't seen any alcohol since leaving Marrakech. Apparently Morocco wasn't the only Muslim country where you could buy a drink.

"Um, I don't really drink," Otto said.

Otto had gotten in trouble for a lot of things, but partying had never been one of them. He didn't really have anything against alcohol, but his mom and dad were both drunks and would fight when they drank. He knew most people didn't get like that, but the thought of drinking always reminded him of shouting matches at his parents' house.

"Oh, one little drink will not hurt you," Nadya said and wagged a slim forefinger at him. "And don't go complaining about your sick stomach. Alcohol is a disinfectant. It will be good for you."

Otto chuckled. "I've never heard that line before."

Nadya handed him one of the beers. It was some European brand he didn't recognize. At least it wasn't a local beer. Grunt had once told him, "Never drink booze made in a Muslim country, pyro. They just don't know how to make it right." Seemed to make sense.

"Are you sure these are okay?" Otto asked. The cap on his beer was a bit bent, like it had come off and been jammed on again.

"These came all the way from Holland. Of course they are going to be battered."

"Well, you came all the way from Russia, and you look fine," Otto said.

As soon as the words came out of his mouth, he wanted to slap himself. What kind of a line was that?

"Oh, you are sweet," she said with a smile. She pulled a Swiss Army knife out of her pocket, flicked open the bottle opener, and popped off the caps.

Otto took a beer from her, feeling deeply confused. He couldn't deny that he felt attracted to her, and she certainly seemed to be hitting on him, but he felt bad about Jaxon. Sure, she had these mood swings and kept ditching him to go off and do her own thing, but they were an item, right?

Well, one beer with a friend wasn't cheating.

"Nosdrovia," she said. "It means 'health' in Russian. It's our way of saying 'cheers.'"

"Nosdrovia," he replied. They clinked their bottles together.

"You have a talent for languages, Otto."

Otto took a sip. The beer was nice and cold. She must have bought them right around the corner. A cold drink felt good in this heat.

"So tell me about the cave paintings. I wish I could see them."

Otto chose his words carefully. "Oh, they just showed a bunch of people gathered together and a city of some kind."

He decided not to mention the triple walls of Atlantis or the ships sailing across the sea. Nadya was a friend, but Grunt had told him again and again not to talk about their mission. As he put it, even if someone you told could be trusted, the next person they talked to might be hostile.

"It was really faint, not much to see, actually," he added, and took another sip to hide his discomfort.

"Were there ruins nearby? There usually are."

"Um, yeah, there were some bits of old pottery and stuff. Not much. Dad was a bit disappointed. It didn't look like an important site at all."

"I bet he took a lot of pictures anyway."

"Oh no, Dr. Yamazaki did," he said.

Damn, you keep slipping up!

Relax, she's a friend.

Nadya smiled and put a hand on his knee. "I sure would like to see those pictures, Otto. They are on her computer, yes? Which room is Dr. Yamazaki's?"

"Um, why are you so interested?" Otto asked. This was getting weird.

As he turned to look at her, the room spun.

"Uh-oh, I think I'm still sick."

"No, you are not sick. Perhaps you are just not used to the beer. Which room is Dr. Yamazaki's?"

Nadya tightened her grip on his knee. The whole room rocked, and the beer bottle seemed to bend in his hand.

"What's going on?" Otto said.

He fell back on the bed, the ceiling spinning

above him. He heard Nadya's voice. It echoed like it came from the end of a long tunnel.

"Never mind, Otto. You rest. I will find her computer. You said you had all the rooms on this wing, yes? That is not too many to break into."

Otto felt himself sinking. A heavy darkness pressed down on top of him like being buried under a dozen quilts.

The darkness felt like it lasted a long, long time.

Gradually awareness returned. The first sensation he felt was a numbing cold.

The next sensation he felt was something digging into his wrists. His hands were behind his back, crossed over one another. He tried to separate them and found he couldn't.

Had Nadya tied him up?

Otto opened his eyes, but everything looked blurry.

Blearily he raised his head and tried to focus.

He sat on the concrete floor of what looked like a cellar, with only a small, boarded-up window high on the wall. His back rested against the bare concrete wall. It was damp and chill. Timbuktu was so hot that even rooms like this always felt warm except in the middle of the night. How long had he been out?

About ten feet away on the other side of the

room, Yuhle sat with his back against the other wall. His hands were behind his back too, and his ankles were bound with thin ropes to one another.

Otto looked down at his own legs and found they were tied too.

He looked back at Yuhle.

The scientist was glaring at him. He had a black eye, and his shirt was torn.

"Smooth move, Romeo," Yuhle growled.

CHAPTER 11

AUGUST 15, 2016, MARRAKECH,
MOROCCO
4:30 A.M.

Grunt had revised his earliest estimation. This was now officially, undeniably the number-one messed-up situation he'd ever been in.

Alone in a hostile environment? Check.

Dying? Check.

No medical care in sight? Check.

Being hunted by enemies? Check.

No way to communicate with his team? Check.

He'd never been able to check all the boxes

before. Four out of five, sure, but not all five. That was a personal best.

Or worst.

Grunt staggered through the darkened streets of Marrakech. Few people were out at this hour except for cops, and he couldn't afford to get caught by the cops. That would get him medical care but also a jail cell and too many questions. Plus with General Meade's global connections, it wouldn't take long before he ended up in that guy's clutches.

So he kept to the back streets, more out of instinct than to keep out of sight. His vision had grown blurry, and he couldn't trust his arms and legs much anymore. He'd lost his cell phone somewhere along the line too. At least he still clutched the pipe he had scrounged. Any weapon was better than no weapon. He'd dropped that, too, a few minutes back and had nearly fainted when he bent over to retrieve it.

He was getting clumsy. Sloppy. If someone got like that in the field, they generally wound up dead.

Pretty soon now, old buddy, he thought as he stumbled and hit his shoulder against a wall.

Hell with that. Keep going.

He came to a small square and looked around in

the dim light of a single underpowered streetlamp. No one. Good.

Was he still going the right way? He knew the Marrakech medina like the back of his hand, knew lots of the old cities of North Africa. But he could barely stand, let alone think. He had to trust his instincts to get him where he needed to go.

He staggered across the square, not bothering to cling to the shadows but taking the quickest route right across the center. He didn't have much time left.

A pair of shadows detached themselves from the greater darkness of a doorway.

Damn, I'm slipping. Making mistakes.

He heard them whispering to each other in Arabic.

"He's a Westerner. Is he drunk?"

"He looks hurt."

"Someone got to him before us."

"Maybe not. Let's check."

Grunt rounded on them, raising his pipe. It was a miracle he didn't fall over.

"Want to see what color your brains are?" he bellowed.

The two bolted.

Grunt continued on his way. That line always

worked. He had gotten it from a Libyan street fighter. Scary guy but a good man to have at your side. Why think of him right now? His mind kept going back to the past. He needed to think of the present. In the brief time he had turned around, he'd seen in the harsh glare of the streetlamp a grisly trail of spots behind him. His blood. He'd patched himself up, but the walk across town had opened one or more wounds. That wasn't as worrying as the internal bleeding. He could feel himself draining out. That was what would kill him before the sun rose.

Grunt shuddered. He hadn't felt fear in a long time, not real fear. The adrenaline rush of battle was fear tempered by a lifetime of training and turned into survival instinct. But now he felt real fear. He had a wound he could not treat that would kill him before he ever got to see the sun again.

Sadness washed over him. The sunrises and sunsets in Africa were like nowhere else in the world. The haze of all the dust kicked up in this dry climate dissipated the sun's slanting rays to make a brilliant display of a thousand different shades of red. It was no wonder the Muslims timed two of their five daily prayers for sunrise and sunset. Who wouldn't want to bow down to such beauty?

He'd missed last night's sunset, curled up in pain and stitching his own wounds with nothing more than a fistful of aspirin as an anesthetic. And now he wasn't going to see another one.

He wouldn't see another sunrise either. His last hour on earth would be spent in darkness.

No defeatism. Keep moving, soldier.

His goal was to get to Ahmad Chukri's. He still had a long way to go, too long. But if he made it, he might just be saved. The guy had more underworld connections than anyone else he knew. If anyone could get a meatball surgeon to operate on a wounded foreigner in the middle of the night with no questions asked, it would be Ahmad Chukri.

The question was—could he afford the price?

He had to get there first, and at this rate, it would take at least another couple of hours. He didn't have another couple of hours.

Despair threatened to drag him down. He'd never make it.

Otto needs you.

He forced himself to keep going.

And then a low, pulsing noise caught his attention. It sounded unusual for this part of town and this time of the night. It wasn't the distant rumble of trucks on one of the bigger roads nearby or the almost silent scrabbling of stray cats through the trash heaped up in a corner. No, it was a low throbbing, rhythmic. Music?

That meant people, and that meant danger.

Most of the time. But at the moment, people offered an opportunity.

Grunt got an idea. It wasn't a very good idea, in fact it was a long shot, but he didn't have many options at this point. While he'd never been a gambling man, he knew that now was the time to roll the dice.

He followed the sound. In his dizziness and confusion, it took some time to find the source, but at last, he ended up against a blank metal door. A thudding beat of house music came from the others side, and the loud conversation of drunken youth. A rave in Marrakech? Not his first choice for recruiting some help, but beggars couldn't be choosers.

He tried the door. Locked, of course. This party was no doubt illegal. For a Muslim country, the Moroccan authorities were pretty lax about drinking and partying, but there were limits.

Time to make a grand entrance. Grunt summoned up the last of his strength and gave the door a kick right next to the lock.

The lock and door frame shattered. The door

whipped open with a bang to reveal a small, packed dance floor under a pulsing red light. The dance floor was surrounded by tables where men sat with bottles of beer and glasses of hard liquor.

The music pounded in his ears. God, how he hated this new electronic junk! No guitars, no singing, no one even composed this stuff. They just mixed up real musicians' tunes and ruined them. No way in Hell he was going to die with this stuff torturing his ears.

"SHUT OFF THAT DAMN NOISE!" he bellowed.

The music stopped. Everyone stared at him in silence.

Grunt surveyed the crowd, trying to focus. All men. No Muslim woman would come to a place like this. Most of the guys looked young, in their teens or early twenties. They all wore the tight jeans and leather jackets that were the universal fashion among young Moroccan men. They studied him nervously. Grunt stumbled down the two steps leading inside, nearly falling, and ended up on the dance floor. The dancers moved back. He took a slow turn about the room, studying everyone. Besides cutting off the music, no one had made a move or said a thing, too astonished by the sudden appearance of a huge, bloodstained foreigner wielding a metal pipe.

"No, this ain't a raid, although it should be," Grunt said in Arabic. "Crap music and no girls. What kind of nightlife is this? Otto would probably love it, though. The loser. God, I miss him."

Grunt spotted a likely prospect sitting alone at a table with a bottle of beer in front of him. Older, not as cocky as the youths but more confident. Also looked slightly better off. The club's drug dealer? Grunt hated his kind, but it was just the kind he needed. He stumbled over to the table. The man rose, gripping the neck of his beer bottle, ready to use it as a weapon.

Grunt batted it aside. The bottle landed on the concrete floor with a crash. He grabbed the startled man by the collar and asked, "You know Ahmad Chukri?"

The man's eyes narrowed. "Who wants to know?"

"He'll give you a thousand euros if you get me there alive."

The man studied him. He opened his mouth, and Grunt knew he was about to haggle for the price.

The guy never got the chance, because at that

moment, Grunt pitched backward onto the nearest table, unconscious.

Grunt's first reaction to waking up was surprise. He did not think that would happen. Living was a good start, though. It opened up all sorts of options.

A hazy glow slowly resolved itself into a light bulb on a ceiling. Grunt blinked, turned his head. A young Moroccan man sitting in a chair by the wall looked up from his phone and took notice. Grunt recognized him as one of Ahmad Chukri's henchmen.

What was the guy's name again? Mubarak? Mabruki? Mumbo jumbo?

Whatever his name was, he hurried out of the room. Grunt drifted off to sleep again. He felt no pain, just the sweet floating buzz of proper painkillers. He had made it. Whatever might happen to him in the next few hours or days, he'd gotten over the first hurdle. He was alive. Maybe he'd even see the sun again.

When he woke up a second time, it was to an older, professional-looking man with salt-and-pepper hair and wire glasses fixing a needle into his arm. A blood packet hung from a metal stand by his bed. Blearily he looked down and saw he was naked. All his wounds were freshly stitched up and professionally bandaged. From his side, where those maniac twins had gutted him, a tube led to another plastic packet half full of what looked like strawberry smoothie. More strawberry smoothie dripped through the tube into it.

"Drawing out the internal bleeding?" Grunt asked.

"Pardon?" the man asked in Arabic.

Grunt realized he had asked the question in English. He thought for a moment and translated the question.

"You taking out the blood from the cut?" he didn't know how to say "internal bleeding" in Arabic. He'd have to learn that sometime. It might come up again.

"Yes. Try to stay still."

"No problem. I can put off yoga class until tomorrow. What's your name, doc?"

"No foolish questions, please."

"Oh, right. The drugs, sorry. How am I?"

"In terrible condition. I have stopped the internal bleeding, and I am giving you blood, but you must not move for several days," the doctor said as he shone a penlight into one eye and then the other.

"Several days? I have places to be."

"The only place you need to be is here. Don't

talk, please." The doctor placed a stethoscope on Grunt's chest, listened for a time, then shook his head and put his instrument away.

"Is it bad?" Grunt asked.

"Very bad. But you will live if you do as I say."

Grunt gave him a grin. "Usually when people say that to me, they have a gun to my head."

The doctor didn't look at all shocked.

"I have no doubt that is true," he replied.

Ahmad Chukri's cheerful voice rang through the room. "Ah, my friend! I have another surprise visit from you!"

The arms dealer spoke in English, obviously so the doctor wouldn't understand. That was fine by Grunt. It seemed fine by the doctor too. The guy was looking at Grunt with obvious distaste.

"The man you commanded to take you here did his job well. Your money belt was untouched."

"I bet it's lighter now," Grunt said.

"Well, there was a certain matter of the doctor's fee, and the door of the nightclub you destroyed, and the thousand euros you offered the man who brought you here. It was a thousand, yes?"

"That's right."

"Ah, so he dealt with you honestly! I thought so. I had the feeling that he wanted to make a good impression on me. Perhaps we will do business sometime."

"I thought you didn't deal in drugs."

"What? Oh no, he isn't a drug dealer. Is that what you thought? No, he deals in stolen cars."

"At an illegal rave?"

"Where better to have a conversation that won't be overheard?"

"Whatever. Do I have any money left?"

The arms dealer shook his head with a smile. "Not much, no. But don't worry about that now. You need to rest, and you are welcome to stay here until you are recovered. We have done much good business together, and I hope to do more."

"Thanks, Ahmad, but I got to get going. Can you get me a computer, so I can reserve a flight?"

Ahmad raised his hands in the air.

"Ah, Malcolm," he said, using one of Grunt's old aliases, "take a look at yourself. You are not going anywhere. You are *hors de combat*, as the French say. Down for the count. Kaput."

"Can't be," Grunt muttered. "I got things to do."

The doctor checked the bandages. Ahmad looked at Grunt's wounds, his face growing serious.

"Those cuts look like they were done with a razor."

"A whole bunch of razors, actually. The bastards even threw them, and their accuracy was terrifying."

"They were twins? Englishmen?"

Grunt stared. "How did you know that?"

Ahmad smiled. There was no humor in the expression. "It is my business to know these things. They are hired assassins. I do not know their names, but they are famous in the business."

"Yeah, I guess you know lots of assassins. You have some nice sniper's rifles."

"I do, not that they would ever buy any. They are famous for attacking with straight razors. Some say they used to be barbers in London."

"Good thing I shave my head myself. I wouldn't want to go to their barbershop."

"They mostly work in Europe, from what I hear, and sometimes in Africa. They've been to Morocco before, and Tunisia. Perhaps more places."

Grunt shook his head, remembering. "One of them waited in my room with a gun. As soon as he didn't hit me with his first shot, he switched to the razor. Weird. He had a better chance with the gun, especially because he had his brother as backup. It was like he'd been ordered to shoot me and decided to do it his way."

"They are madmen to switch to an inferior weapon when faced with someone like you."

"Yeah, well, they nearly got me anyway. I owe you one, and I owe that car thief one too. I guess the Bard was wrong about there being no honor among thieves."

"The Bard?"

"Shakespeare. Haven't you ever read him?"

"No. Have you ever read Ferdowsi?"

"Who's that?"

"Our Shakespeare."

"Whatever. Do you know anything else about these maniacs?"

"Only two things. I heard a strange story from one customer. He said he worked with those twins on a job. They had to sneak through a forest to get to the target, some man in a house they needed to kill. My customer had worked with those two before and said they had always been fearless. But this time as they went through the forest, they saw a bee, and you know what the twins did? They fled in terror! From just one little bee."

"Afraid of bees, eh? Not sure how that's going to be useful."

Ahmad shrugged. "You never know. All information is useful information."

"True enough. What's the second thing you know?"

Instead of answering, he turned to the doctor and switched to Arabic. "Is this man healthy enough to travel?"

The doctor, who was putting his instruments away in a black medical bag, clicked his tongue and said, "Certainly not. He might die if he moves in the next few days."

"Ahmad, what's going on?" Grunt asked in English to cut the doctor out of the conversation again.

The arms dealer looked grim. "You are not going to like it."

"Tell me."

Ahmad sighed. "The twins have left Marrakech. I do not know where they went, but I suspect they're—"

"Heading for the rest of the team," Grunt said, sitting up in bed. Pain lanced through his side, making him gasp.

The doctor put a gentle hand on his chest. "Lie down. You are not fit to go anywhere."

"My team needs me."

"In this state, you cannot help them," Ahmad said.

"I'm going. Get me a computer so I can book the first flight south," Grunt said, swinging his feet over the side of the bed and grabbing his clothes from the bedside table. The pain was intense, cutting through the drugs.

He ignored it. He had a duty to perform.

CHAPTER 12

AUGUST 15, 2016, THE DESERT OUTSIDE
TIMBUKTU
7:30 A.M.

Hold your position and wait for reinforcements. Hold your position and wait for reinforcements.

That had always been her least favorite order in the Special Forces. She wasn't the kind of person to sit around and do nothing when there was action going down.

Isadore Grant paced around the little camp she and Brett had set up in the desert twenty miles north of Timbuktu. Two small tents stood nestled in a sandy swale between a pair of low, rocky hills. The position was too open and exposed for her liking, but it was the best they could find in this featureless desert.

A few hundred yards to the north, a rented Land Rover stood parked in a cluster of bushes with a small tent next to it. The roof of the Land Rover poked above the tops of the bushes and gleamed in the sunlight, visible from a good distance away. That was the distraction. Hopefully if the Russians tracked her here, they'd attack that camp and give her some warning. Considering their level of training, that little trick probably wouldn't work.

After getting attacked in her hotel the first night she had arrived, Isadore knew the Russians were in the thick of this mess. They obviously had a whole team here.

Did they know about Jaxon and the Atlantis Allegiance, or were they simply spying on the largest Atlantean community in North Africa?

Whatever they were up to, they were certainly on the ball. They'd heard of her arrival and assembled an assault team within hours. When she had reported in to General Corbin, he had told her to get out of town and wait until she got reinforcements.

All he had said was "the twins are coming." He didn't need to say any more.

The McKay twins. She shuddered. No one creeped her out more than those two, not even the chemically created zombie teenager sharing her camp.

He lay on the hill to the north, as still as a stone, watching the surrounding countryside. He'd been up there for hours and would remain there for years if she didn't tell him otherwise. The perfect sentry. Good in a fight too. He sure had helped when the Russians came bursting through the door. So far, field testing of the artificially created Atlanteans was going well. An army of these creatures would be unstoppable.

Isadore opened up her laptop and adjusted a small satellite dish linked to the computer. The dish was tuned to pick up the narrowband frequency of a CIA satellite. General Corbin had given her the access codes even though she wasn't CIA, and that counted as treason. He was helpful that way. Once she logged in, she began to search all the intelligence about the region, especially regarding Russian involvement. Usually she did this before setting out on a mission, but General Corbin had sent her out at the last minute, and she had thought she only had to deal with the Atlantis Allegiance. Now it was obvious there were larger forces at work.

During the Cold War from the 1950s to the end of the 1980s, the Soviet Union had rivaled the United States for world domination. Part of that rivalry had involved collecting allies in the developing world. The Soviets had spent a lot of money in Africa on aid and sold large numbers of weapons to various dictators. The United States and other Western powers did the same. About half of Africa supported the old Soviet Union, while the other half supported the West. After the collapse of the Soviet Union, the new Russia had financial troubles and internal unrest to occupy its attention, and aid to Africa dried up. Many former "socialist" African countries aligned themselves with the West and became "capitalist democracies," although really most were still the same dictatorships or corrupt pseudodemocracies. Only the names and the alliances had changed.

So Russian influence in Africa had waned in the 1990s and early 2000s. They still sold lots of weapons, but so did everybody else. American influence waned too. The Americans had mostly been in Africa as a proxy fight against the Soviets. When that stopped, the Americans focused more on the Middle

East, where oil and an alliance with Israel had always made the region a priority.

Then the Chinese moved in, sending thousands of engineers to Africa to help with infrastructure projects while also getting mining concessions. Soon the Chinese were everywhere, investing and building and making themselves out to be valuable economic partners to every African leader. They had been the most practical of the three big powers. With the end of the Cold War, they had seen an opening and an opportunity. Now African raw materials supplied China's industrial boom. Chinese development projects in Africa brought in money and influence. China was even buying agricultural land to feed its giant population. On a continent where food shortages and even famine were regular problems, corrupt African leaders were selling their best farmland to foreigners.

Isadore shrugged. It made no difference to her. What she was really interested in was how much the Russians and the Chinese were involved in Mali and the surrounding countries.

According to the CIA database, China didn't have much investment in the Saharan countries. Not enough money or raw materials in it for them. They sold arms and had spies, of course, but according to the latest CIA intelligence, they weren't a major factor in this region. There was also no evidence of their interest in the People of the Sea. The Chinese considered themselves the world's oldest and greatest civilization, so it probably never occurred to them that the stories of Atlantis could be true. It would certainly hurt Chinese pride to know that another civilization had them beat by a few thousand years.

So the Chinese weren't going to be a problem on this mission. The Russians were a different story. Besides the usual level of spies that they deployed in every country, they had a large number of archaeologists. That was interesting. Archaeologists in sensitive regions of the world often doubled as secret agents. Most of the time, they were real scientists doing real research, but the fact that they traveled extensively in the world's hotspots and knew the locals made them very useful to their governments. America, Russia, the UK, France, Germany—all intelligence agencies of the major powers had archaeologists on the payroll. Some were only part-time spies who just happened to have a legitimate research interest in a sensitive region, while others were trained fighters given a bit of archaeological education and sent on specific missions.

Several Russian archaeological teams worked in Mauritania and Mali. Right here in Timbuktu, there was Dimitri Rublev, a linguist who the CIA database flagged as suspected KGB. Plus the database listed a couple of Russian archaeological teams excavating abandoned settlements in the desert just outside of town. Isadore suspected that her attackers had come from those archaeological teams.

Another detail caught her interest. The Russians ran a large archaeological survey in Mauritania looking for rock art. This whole region had a long history of cave paintings dating back millennia. Interesting enough from a scientific standpoint, but why would the Russians care?

She checked on the survey and found that it was quite well funded by something called the Russian Academy for International History, which she knew the KGB used as a front for various projects around the world.

Isadore got up and paced around her little camp, now and then glancing at Brett, who still lay in the same position on watch atop the nearby hill.

The Russians had several teams scouring the Mauritanian desert. They'd found numerous cave paintings and had published several scientific articles on the subject, but that obviously was not what they were really after. So what were they looking for? Old Atlantean settlements, perhaps? But there was no evidence of any Russian interest in the modern Atlantean population. The ambush in her hotel room had been more of a reaction. She had shown up, and suddenly the Russians took notice. They probably didn't know why she was here but decided to get rid of her anyway. If she hadn't appeared, she suspected, they would have continued their quiet research into the Atlantean past.

That didn't make any sense. Why wouldn't they be interested in the living Atlanteans? Those were the potential soldiers, not the dried-up bones of their ancestors. But the Russians were too practical to spend so much money unless they thought there would be some solid benefit. They obviously thought there was something in the Atlanteans' past that was more useful than the people alive today.

What could that be?

Also, the Russians were too professional not to have noticed the arrival of Jaxon and her pals. They'd be spying on them by now.

Another detail had caught her eye in the Mauritania CIA report. It was a new and vague report, coming secondhand from some local sources. The Mauritanian government had rounded up all the

People of the Sea and taken them to an unknown location. She sent Corbin a message asking him to dig for more information.

In the meantime, she would do her own digging. Perhaps she needed to strap this Dimitri fellow to a chair and question him. And maybe one of those archaeologists in Mauritania as well.

The Atlantis Allegiance had driven through Mauritania to get here. Had they met up with the Russians? Were they in league with them? Had Jaxon and her friends been searching in the desert for something too?

Maybe things would get clearer once the McKay twins made it here and they could go on the offensive.

In the meantime, there was nothing to do but wait. Isadore limbered up, going through her intense daily exercise routine of yoga for flexibility, pushups and sit-ups for strength, and lifting a few rocks to tone her muscles. She missed her home gym, and she missed being able to go to the shooting range. She didn't dare squeeze off any rounds out here. She didn't want to attract any attention.

A low whistle from the hill told her they had attracted attention anyway. Brett was signaling to her.

He made a series of quick hand signals using a system she had taught him from her old Special Forces days. He held up two fingers and pointed to the left and to the right, then pulled his hand back. Two enemies were converging on the Land Rover from opposite flanks. Good, the Russians had actually fallen for her little ruse. Brett held his two hands together, the forefinger of one hand touching the wrist of the other. The attackers carried assault rifles. Great. A firefight was just what she needed to relieve the tedium.

Isadore grabbed her own AK-47. It wasn't her first choice of weapon, and it wasn't in the greatest of condition, but it was the best she could get on such short notice. She didn't know any arms dealers in Timbuktu, so she'd had to mug a prosperous store-owner and take his. That was one of the nice things about this part of the world. Everybody who was anybody carried a gun.

She was about to run up the hill and get into position to fire down on the Russians when she paused. Only two? There had been more than that in her hotel room, and surely they would send more than just two to fight a battle all the way out here.

Maybe they hadn't fallen for her trick after all. Maybe the guys down at the Land Rover were a distraction to keep her eyes away from the real attack.

She crouched. Scanned the surrounding terrain. To her north stood the hill on which Brett lay in watch and beyond it the Land Rover and the two Russians. To the south rose another hill, a bit smaller. Both were stony and pretty much bare. Not much cover there. To the west and east, the land was sandy and more open. A few low dunes and the occasional bush provided some cover.

Which way would they come?

The glint of reflected sunlight to the east made her hit the dirt. To her surprise, no shot came. Had the sun caught the barrel of a gun or the glass of some binoculars? Had they seen Brett as well as her?

The reflection had come from the top of a low dune about four hundred yards away. It did not repeat, and she saw no one.

Then their plan became obvious, because it was what she herself would do if attacking a position like this. The guy hiding behind that dune was not a sniper, as she had initially feared, but a spotter equipped with a radio to contact two teams—the one hitting the fake campsite and the one moving in from the south behind the cover of that hill. A classic pincer movement.

She looked at Brett, who was studying the movements of the two approaching the Land Rover and fake campsite. After a moment, he turned in her direction. She signaled him to stay put, pointed in the direction of the threat, and ran a finger across her throat. Brett didn't have any weapons, but with the serum he'd been given, he was his own weapon. He'd just have to figure out how to kill those guys himself.

She'd have her own hands full with the group coming from the south.

She crawled across the narrow valley and worked her way up the side of the southern hill, keeping behind rocks and worming her way through little depressions as much as she could. The spotter might notice her movement, but there was no helping it. If she didn't get to the top of the hill before the enemy, she was done for.

She had studied this hill when they had first camped here. It was a steep-sided spine of rock with very little level space on top of it. She couldn't see anything of the other side until she was at the very summit.

Isadore made it to the top without getting shot at. Before exposing herself, she glanced over her shoulder in Brett's direction. He had disappeared.

She heard no shots, no shouts, only the wind blowing through the desert, shifting the sands with a soft hiss.

She peeked over a rock at the other side of the hill and ducked back as a bullet cracked off the stone inches from her face.

Isadore shifted her position five yards to the right and popped up from cover. She had just enough time to see three men in a triangle formation ascending the back side of the hill. The one in front had been the one who shot at her. She snapped off an aimless shot that winged him in the shoulder, then dropped back down before the other two could fire.

Okay, this was a problem. She was outnumbered two to one, and the third guy might still have enough in him to put up a fight. Plus there was the Brett situation. She might have to bail him out. From the brief glimpse she'd gotten of the men, they looked trained and fit, probably the same professionals who had attacked her in her hotel room.

The odds of her getting out of this were slim. She grinned. God, she had missed this!

Shifting her position again, she dared another glimpse over the summit of the hill. Now she only saw two of them. The front man, who had spilled some blood on the stones around him, ducked out of sight as soon as she appeared. The one to his right and a little behind had moved farther to the right. The one to the left had disappeared.

Great, they were spreading out, trying to flank her and fire at her from both sides.

She took a shot at the guy to the right and missed. The man fired back, his AK-47 making a distinctive bark, and the bullet buzzed over her head. They exchanged another couple of shots, but both were too well protected, and neither of them hit.

Then the wounded front man plucked up enough courage to add his fire to the fight. He moved too slowly, though, and Isadore took him out with a well-placed shot to the forehead.

"One down, five to go, assuming there aren't any more lurking around here," she muttered.

She kept exchanging fire with the man on the right, but he'd chosen a good spot and had enough training to fire quickly and get back down. Isadore bit her lip. They were too evenly matched, and this guy was wasting her time while his buddy moved around to her left. In another minute, he'd be in a good spot, and it would be all over.

Time to change the script.

She scrambled a few feet down the back slope of the hill and sprinted along it to her left for several yards then fell prone and listened.

Silence. No sound from Brett's side of the battle. What was going on over there?

But then there came the scrabbling of someone crawling over the loose rock and sand. It was very faint, and someone who hadn't trained their senses could have easily missed it. This guy moved like a pro.

Plus he was close, really close.

Isadore eased herself into a better position, making no sound. She leveled her assault rifle, sighting down the barrel, becoming one with the weapon as she had so many times before. He'd be quick, but he'd have the disadvantage of moving first. She lay in wait like a tiger, ready to pounce.

He popped up, lightning fast, a full five feet to the right of where Isadore had last heard him.

Damn, he was good.

Not good enough. A split second before he could fire, Isadore's bullet punctured his neck. He fell back, choking and clutching at the fatal wound.

A bullet cracked off the rock at her feet, sending painful shards into her leg.

Where had that come from?

The guy on the right had hustled up and lay at the top of the hill, firing along its length at her. All she had for protection was a thin rise of rock. She squeezed behind it as another bullet whizzed by.

Desperately she looked around. Clear hillside all around. If she moved out of this meager shelter, she'd be dead in an instant.

She was trapped.

Daring another peek from behind her meager shield, she saw something that made her even more worried. The spotter was running into the valley with a high-powered rifle. As soon as he got into the right position, he'd be able to pick her off at leisure, and there wasn't a thing she could do about it.

Time to move.

She switched the AK-47 to full auto, lifted it above the rock, and sprayed the hilltop with unaimed fire. Then she burst from her cover to sprint to a boulder some five yards away.

She barely got to her feet before she had to throw herself back down again. The guy on the hilltop had guts. He hadn't even dropped down at the burst and had waited for her to expose herself. It was a miracle she hadn't been hit.

Now she was in the same position as before. The rifleman in the valley wouldn't take more than another ten, maybe fifteen seconds to get into position, and then it would be "Good night, Isadore."

A cry from the valley made her cock her head. That sounded like someone getting hit, but she hadn't heard a gunshot.

She peeked out from behind her shelter and had to duck back as the guy on the hilltop fired, but she had time to see enough. The rifleman in the valley lay on the ground, blood pouring from his head.

The man on the hilltop fired again, but not at her.

She glanced over at the other hill. Brett was dodging the bullets, leaping from side to side like a game of hopscotch, except each jump took him several feet. He moved erratically, not in a regular pattern, to keep the Russian from being able to hit him. Then Brett fell into a roll, leapt up with a rock in his hand, and threw it.

It sailed across the valley almost too fast to see, ending its trajectory with a sickening crunch.

Isadore peeked from behind her cover again. The Russian lay dead, his head a bloody pulp.

"Did you get the other two?" Isadore called over.

"Yes," Brett called back. "The same way."

She got up and carefully surveyed the area. No one else seemed to be around, and the three on her hill were all dead.

"Pity we couldn't keep one for questioning," she muttered.

"I did," Brett called over.

Isadore gaped. How could he have heard that?

"You did? How?"

"I threw two rocks, one to break each arm."

"Of course. Silly question. Let's go check him out."

Isadore reloaded her gun, shaking her head. A few more of these artificial Atlanteans running around, and she'd be out of a job. Once she'd loaded up, she trotted over to Brett's position, and he led her to where the two Russians lay near the Land Rover. One was as dead as a doornail. The other lay moaning, both arms bent at unnatural angles.

So Brett figured they should keep a prisoner. That showed initiative, something he hadn't had at first. When he had originally been assigned to her, he was like a sleepwalker, but now some thoughts were going on behind that blank face. Isadore wondered how much more he would wake up.

"Well, well, well," Isadore said, coming up to the Russian and addressing him in his own language. "You're going to tell me what's going on and where your friends are, or I'm going to let my friend have fun with you."

CHAPTER 13

AUGUST 15, 2016, A CELLAR SOMEWHERE
IN THE OUTSKIRTS OF TIMBUKTU
2:00 P.M.

Otto felt miserable. He'd compromised the mission. Not only were he and Dr. Yuhle prisoners, but Nadya and Dimitri had taken all their computers with all the data on the Atlanteans.

And all because he'd been a lonely idiot who got easily seduced by a woman paying some attention to him.

He wasn't going to get any sympathy from Yuhle. Apparently while Otto was unconscious, Nadya had laughingly told the scientist about how he had screwed up. Now all Yuhle did was glare at him.

They'd been stuck down here all day. Twice, a silent, burly guard with a blond buzz cut, no English, and a pistol strapped to his hip had come down to give them some food and water and let them relieve themselves in a bucket. He didn't untie them, though, so eating and peeing had been done in a clumsy, embarrassing fashion that hadn't improved Yuhle's mood.

"Look, we have to get out of here," Otto said after the guard had left a second time. "I have a plan."

"Says the man dribbling down his pants leg," Yuhle grumbled.

"Hard to pee right when you can't hold it, and having that guy open my fly was all the help I was going to ask for."

"Fair enough. So what's your plan, genius?"

"Let's try to untie each other, and then we'll get on either side of the door and make some noise. When the guard comes in, we'll overpower him."

"Did you see that in a movie?"

"Got any better ideas?" Otto snapped. He understood that Yuhle was angry, but they needed to find a way out of this mess.

"Not really. Crawl over here."

Crawling wasn't really an option with his legs tied together and his hands tied behind his back, so Otto rolled. Once he made it across the room, he examined Yuhle's bonds. Like him, Yuhle was tied with thin, strong rope. His hands were swollen and white from having the circulation cut off, and livid red scratches became visible anytime the ropes moved a little. Otto was in pain too. Even if they did get the ropes off, it would be a while before they could stand or do anything with their hands.

Already his own hands felt so numb he could barely move his fingers. There was no way he could untie Yuhle's knots. So instead he had the geneticist turn around, and he tried gnawing at the rope with his teeth.

First Otto tried to sink a canine tooth into the knot and work the knot free, but all that did was give him a toothache, so he settled with chewing at the rope. It was natural fiber, not plastic, and it slowly began to give way as he ground it between his teeth.

"You're slobbering all over me," Yuhle grumbled.

"Sorry." Otto's reply came out muffled thanks to his mouthful of rope.

Otto's teeth began to ache. His jaw grew sore, his lips chapped from the friction of the rope, but he could tell he was making progress.

Even so, he had to take a break. His jaw was in agony. He hoped he didn't break a tooth doing this.

"Nadya mentioned that you and Dimitri were celebrating some big discovery. What was that?" he asked.

"Well, I guess I can tell you. You'll blab it to everybody, but since the Russians already know, it can't do any harm."

"Come on," Otto said, feeling hurt.

"Don't look to me for pity, kid. Dimitri and I discovered an old text talking about the healing water, giving the same legend we heard before about it being the original water on Earth before the Flood. This text was a bit different, though. It gave a location."

"Was it the same place we found in Mauritania?"

"You mean the same place Jaxon found? I don't recall you doing anything."

Otto turned away, feeling miserable. He'd lost Yuhle's respect, something he didn't realize he valued until he had lost it. If they ever got out of this alive, he'd lose everyone else's respect too, Jaxon's especially.

There's something to look forward to, he thought bitterly.

Dr. Yuhle went on.

"No, the well is right here in Mali, in an obscure bit of desert in the far north of the country. Back when Timbuktu was a big trading center for caravans crossing the Sahara and heading south into the better lands, there were villages and caravanserai at all the oases."

"Caravanserai?" Otto asked.

"They were like hotels for the caravans. You got shelter, food, feed for your animals, and a mosque to pray in. Most importantly, you got water."

"Sounds like a good business model," Otto said and got back to chewing on Yuhle's ropes.

"It was. Some of them lasted for hundreds of years. Anyway, we found a mention of one of these healing wells right next to a caravanserai. The text named the place, and so now Dimitri is looking through old travelogues and business ledgers from the Middle Ages looking for references to this place. I'm sure it won't take long until he finds the location. Most of these places have been identified by archaeologists."

Otto pulled back, wiping his mouth on his shoulder. He'd chewed through a bit more of the rope but still had a long way to go.

"So they'd find the healing water. Maybe that's what Dimitri was here looking for in the first place."

Yuhle nodded. "I think so. He's obviously working for the Russian government. You were out cold, but I saw the arrangement they have upstairs when they dragged me in. Several guards, weapons, a satellite hookup for their computers, detailed maps of the region, the works. But I never heard any of the locals mention a large group of Russians living here, only Dimitri and your new girlfriend."

"She's not my girlfriend!"

"Whatever. I'm thinking that only the two of them were here, looking for the healing water. Something made them bring a whole team down."

"Us showing up?"

"Maybe. Or maybe something else we haven't learned about yet."

The heavy footsteps of their guard on the stairs outside the locked door told them they were about to get another visit. Otto rolled back to his side of the room, and Yuhle turned his back against the wall.

Otto made it into position an instant before the bolt on the outside of the door snapped open.

The guard came in, this time with Nadya. The Russian woman blew Otto a kiss. Otto blushed.

Yuhle glared. The guard, looking bored, lit a cigarette and stood by the door.

"And how are my two friends doing today?" Nadya asked.

"Peachy," Yuhle said.

Nadya's brow furrowed. "I do not know that expression in English. I will assume it is sarcasm."

"Big time," the geneticist replied.

Nadya strolled over to Yuhle. Otto tensed. What if she checked the ropes tying his hands behind his back? He'd gnawed about a third of the way through. She would be sure to notice that.

"Your computers are password protected with an excellent encryption system," Nadya said.

"Too bad we couldn't encrypt Otto," Yuhle growled.

Nadya looked over her shoulder at Otto and treated him to a smile before turning back to Yuhle. "Do not judge him too harshly. He is a lonely, silly boy far from home, and I am a very attractive woman."

"Not on the inside," Yuhle replied.

"Give me the passwords to your computers."

Yuhle fixed her with a steady gaze. "No."

Nadya pulled a compact automatic pistol from

her pocket, flicked off the safety, and pointed it at Otto.

"Give me the passwords, or I will kill your young friend."

Yuhle paled, but he set his jaw, frowned, and shook his head.

"What are you doing? Give her the passwords!" Otto shouted. He stared at the barrel of the gun, the dark little muzzle seeming to encompass his entire vision, like it was a black hole sucking him in.

"I can't," Yuhle's voice came out strained. "This is bigger than either of us. A whole people is in jeopardy."

Nadya shrugged. "Perhaps you do not value his life after what he did. That is reasonable, but I am sure you value yours."

She pointed the gun at Yuhle. The scientist flinched but, after a moment, sat up straighter.

"No."

Nadya kicked him, making him fall on his side. She knelt with her knee on his neck and the barrel of the gun pressed against his temple.

"You would rather die than give me the passwords?" she asked.

Yuhle turned his eyes up to meet hers. "Kill me. You're not getting those passwords."

Their gaze locked. It held for several long seconds. Otto watched, terrified and fascinated. Understanding seemed to flash between them. It looked almost intimate. Nadya nodded slowly and got up.

"Yes, you would rather die than betray your friends," she said in a voice made soft with respect. She turned to Otto and smiled. "You never know where you will find bravery. Here this little man with the glasses shows more bravery than many soldiers I have met. It is no matter. We have a computer hacker who can break into the computers remotely from Moscow. It will take time. Long enough for your friends to come looking for you and allow us to set a trap for them."

Without another word, she walked out of the room. The guard dropped his cigarette on the concrete floor, crushed it out with his boot, and followed, bolting the door behind him.

Yuhle gasped where he lay on the floor, taking in great gulps of air, his body trembling all over. His glasses had fallen off. Otto rolled over to him.

"Turn around," he said. "We have to get out of here."

Yuhle sat up and turned around, still shaking, and Otto started to chew on the cords again.

"Sorry," Yuhle said.

Otto pulled back. "For what?"

"For telling her she could shoot you."

Otto slumped. "I messed up. I know that."

"That's not what I meant," Yuhle said, shaking his head. "It's bigger than you or me. I was willing to die too. Well, not exactly willing, but more willing to do that than live with the shame of betraying an entire race."

Otto remembered a story Yuhle had told him about his favorite uncle, a cop who had shot an unarmed black teen and bragged about it. And now here he was willing to sacrifice his life for a race most people didn't even know existed. Meanwhile, Otto was flirting with the enemy and getting them all in trouble.

Otto bit harder on the ropes, enraged with himself. Why did he have to be such a screwup? Just because he had parents who didn't give a damn? He was born healthy and living in the First World, while all around him was poverty like he had never seen except on television and a race that his own government was trying to enslave. He didn't have the right to self-pity, and he sure didn't have the right to mess up the mission for everybody else.

A loud crack and a sharp pain woke him up from

his thoughts. He pulled back, felt around his teeth with his tongue. A little hard bit was on the tip of it. He spat it out and stared. A small piece of tooth lay on the floor.

"What's wrong?" Yuhle asked.

"Nothing," Otto muttered.

He felt around his mouth with his tongue. Yeah, he'd chipped off a chunk of one of his incisors. Great. Now if he got out of this alive, he could look forward to a trip to the local dentist's office. He hoped Novocain had made it to this part of the world.

Shifting to the other side of his mouth, he continued to chew.

Ten minutes later, he made it through the ropes, and Yuhle moved his arms with a contented sigh. Falling back exhausted and sore, he watched as the scientist shook off the remnants of the ropes, put on his glasses with fumbling hands, and stared at Otto.

"Your mouth is all bloody."

"I believe it."

Yuhle flexed his fingers and shook his hands, trying to get the circulation back in them. After a minute, he worked on the ropes that tied his legs.

"Hurry up. If they come down now, we're sunk," Otto said.

"I'm trying, but I can barely feel my hands, and the only thing I can feel is pain."

After a minute, he finally got the knot untied. Then he got to work on Otto. After a couple of minutes, he was free. Otto rubbed his wrists and hands, trying to get the blood to flow back into them.

"Good job," Yuhle said, standing up. His legs were so cramped that he had to lean on the wall for support. "Now all we have to deal with is a locked door and several trained killers."

"Piece of cake," Otto said with a sigh.

They both looked around the small cellar. It had been completely cleaned out, and there was nothing they could use as a weapon. Otto picked up a length of rope about three feet long and held it, feeling lame. Grunt could probably kill a dozen ninjas with it. God, he missed that guy.

"So now what?" Otto asked Yuhle. He had a piece of rope in his hands too.

"We need to get out of here and either get away with the computers or destroy them before the Russians kill us. We can't let them get that information. Dr. Yamazaki's computer, and mine too, have the entire Atlantean genetic sequence on them, not to mention the location of the well Jaxon found, all the pictures we took of it, and the contact information of all the people who have helped us."

"Like that old professor outside Tucson?"

"Exactly. You want him to get killed too?"

"No, let's do this."

Yuhle looked at a loss. "How?"

"We can pretend to get in an argument. Start shouting at me about messing up with Nadya, and I'll start swearing back at you."

Yuhle snorted. "That only works in the movies."

"Well, we have to get them down here somehow."

Yuhle looked uncertainly at the door. "Let's start shouting for help, like we're panicking. Actually, only you do that. It will be more believable from you. Once you start, I'll shout at you to shut up."

Otto sighed, his heart beating fast. "All right, but one thing."

"What?"

"If you get out alive and I don't, don't tell them how I messed up."

Yuhle studied him a moment. His scowl softened a little. "All right."

Otto turned to the door and bellowed, "Help! Help us! They've taken us prisoner! Call the police!"

Yuhle backed away so he'd be behind the door

when it opened. Otto had another thought and got down on the ground, winding the rope around his feet and putting his hands behind his back. He kicked the door with his feet.

"Help us! Police!"

"Quiet!" Yuhle bellowed. "You'll get us in trouble!"

Footsteps stomped down the stairway on the other side of the door. The bolt slid back, and the door opened.

The guard stormed in, shouting something at Otto in Russian and getting ready to kick him.

Just then, Yuhle snuck up behind him and put the rope around his neck. He pulled, sticking a knee in the small of the guard's back to get some leverage as he strangled him.

The guard's eyes bugged out in pain and surprise. Otto yanked the rope from around his legs and scrambled to his feet.

The guard remained surprised for only a moment. In a lightning-fast move that Otto didn't fully see, he managed to twist around, knock Yuhle's knee away, and flip him so he landed with a thud on the floor. His glasses skittered away.

Otto used his rope like a whip and smacked the guard across the face, catching him in the eye. As

Otto wound up for another swing, the guard punched him. He was half blinded from the rope, so the punch didn't connect properly, but even a glancing blow on the side of the head sent Otto staggering.

Then the guard's attention got distracted by Yuhle grabbing his legs and trying to pull him down. That didn't happen, but it did get the guard momentarily off balance and bought Otto a precious second to recover.

"Run!" the scientist shouted.

Instead Otto whipped the guard again, only to have him grab the end of the rope and yank it out of Otto's hand.

"Run!" Yuhle repeated, struggling with the man's legs and keeping him immobilized for the moment. "Get the computers. They're more important!"

The desperate command woke Otto up to priorities. He bolted out the door.

Beyond was a flight of bare concrete steps. He raced up them and found himself in a large room that looked like a work area. The first thing he noticed was Dimitri at a table a few feet away, hunched over a map. Also on that table were the laptops of the Atlantis Allegiance, open and connected to heavy cables that led to another laptop that had some sort of program working on it.

Otto didn't have time to see anything else. He ran for Dimitri, who was too startled by Otto's sudden appearance to do anything except stand there and stare until Otto's fist connected with his jaw and sent him tumbling to the floor, unconscious.

Otto looked around. Another table by the wall held some more computers, all switched off, and piles of books and some of Mali's old medieval manuscripts. He glanced at the computer with the program running. All the writing was in the Cyrillic alphabet, and more Russian script was appearing in a dialog pane. A progress bar showed the figure "97%."

Did that mean it was almost done? Was this the computer hacker cracking the codes to the Atlantis Allegiance computers?

A cry of pain from the cellar pushed Otto into action. He pulled the cords out of the Russian computer. The dialog pane and the progress bar froze.

He turned to grab the computers, but at that moment the guard appeared at the top of the stairs. Also, a door opened to his right, and another guard, equally huge and looking equally pissed off, burst in.

They closed in on him, hemming him in as he

backed up to a corner of the room, the laptops clutched to his chest. The guard from the cellar drew his automatic pistol.

This is it, Otto said to himself. *This is how I'm going to die.*

Just then, the dull thud of an explosion echoed from the open door to his right.

CHAPTER 14

AUGUST 15, 2016, TIMBUKTU
4:00 P.M.

Jaxon was frantic. After a brief breakdown in the desert that delayed them a couple of hours while Vivian fixed a cracked radiator cap, they had come back from the refugee camp to find their hotel rooms looted and Yuhle and Otto gone. The man at the front desk had been knocked out from behind and hadn't seen anything. The two had simply vanished, along with all the computers and spare weapons. At least the thieves hadn't gotten the last of the healing water Jaxon had found in the desert. That had been in an ordinary-looking plastic bottle on a shelf, and whoever had robbed them had obviously not thought it was of any value.

Vivian didn't want the police involved, so she gave the hotel worker some shut-up money and tried to call Grunt, who had not checked in for far too long. No answer. That made them even more worried. Helpless to do anything about whatever the trouble might be in Marrakech, Jaxon and Vivian concentrated on the problems in Timbuktu. They had spent the rest of the evening scouring the streets of Timbuktu for any sign of their friends, finally giving up in the small hours of the morning. Then, after sleeping a few hours, they waited until the manuscript museum opened. It was a large, modern building built by the French government to preserve Timbuktu's massive collection of medieval manuscripts. They asked to see Dimitri Rublev. The workers there said he hadn't come in that day and had left early the night before. That struck them as odd, they commented, because he came in every day, usually staying from opening time to closing. "I hope he isn't sick," one curator said.

The museum people offered to call him, but Vivian said no.

"We have to catch them by surprise," Vivian told

Jaxon as they left the building's cool interior and returned to the furnace of the Saharan morning. "We don't want him knowing we're after him."

"What makes you so sure Dimitri was involved?" Jaxon asked.

"I suspected him from the start. I've been asking around about other foreigners in the area. Everyone notices them because there are so few. It turns out there are a lot of Russian researchers working in Mali and Mauritania. Mostly archaeologists and historians like Dimitri."

"You think that the Russian government is after my people too?" Jaxon asked, her heart sinking.

"I wasn't sure before, but I am now," Vivian said, checking her weapons as she drove the Land Rover through the streets of Timbuktu.

Salif was still in the back seat. He had stayed with them after they had dropped off the refugees with the Atlantean community.

"I can have our people check around town," he offered. "We will not be noticed like you will."

"All right," Jaxon replied. "But please hurry. We don't know what they're doing to our friends."

Salif organized a couple dozen Atlanteans to spread out through the small city. They quietly asked around each neighborhood whether a group of

Russians lived in the area. One woman went to the very fringes of the northern edge of town, and there, in a dusty neighborhood looking out over the desert, heard that some foreigners had just rented a house there. The woman took it upon herself to do a bit of spying and came back to report. By then it was midafternoon, and Jaxon was getting increasingly desperate.

"They are in a big concrete house," the woman said. "I saw Nadya, Dimitri's friend, plus many strong men I didn't recognize. I think they are all new arrivals. One always stood by the door smoking, but I think he was really there as a watchman."

Jaxon thanked her and got directions to the place, and she and Vivian set out in the Land Rover. Salif they left behind, not wanting to put the kind Atlantean in harm's way.

"Once we get there, I want you to hang back, honey," Vivian said. She was fully armed and had stuffed some small grenades in the pockets of her jacket. Sweat poured down her face, but she had put on the extra clothing because she needed the pockets.

"You can't go in there alone!"

"I don't see what choice I have. At least I have some stun grenades. Thank God I brought some along to the refugee camp. Whoever broke into our rooms took all the rest. I don't even have enough ammo for this fight."

"I can help. I'm Atlantean," Jaxon objected. "I'm stronger and faster than you are."

"And you have no military training and are too valuable to lose."

Jaxon remembered how Vivian had crept away while they were dying in the desert, so Jaxon could have the last of their water. When she had found the mercenary lying nearly unconscious in the sand, she had said the same thing about Jaxon being more important.

"I'm not buying that this time," Jaxon objected. "We have to save Yuhle and Otto, and the only way we can do that is to work together."

Vivian shook her head, a lock of her long blond hair falling out of her headscarf.

"No," she said. It sounded final.

Jaxon bit her lip. If Vivian thought she was going to sit back and do nothing while her friends were in danger, she had another thing coming.

But what could she do? Jaxon felt a sudden rush of fear. What good was a bit of strength and speed when faced with guns?

They passed through the crowded center of

Timbuktu with its adobe mosques and old homes to a newer area. The buildings, mostly ugly concrete blocks, stood more widely apart. Goats nibbled on sparse grass in the open, windblown lots between them. Through gaps in the buildings, they could see where the neighborhood ended and the land opened up into desert. The afternoon sun shone harshly on the brown sand and the gray concrete, making everything uncomfortably bright even through the tinted window.

Vivian stopped the Land Rover, and they got out.

"You stay here," the mercenary ordered. "According to the directions that woman gave, the Russians are in a building just around that street corner and to the left. I'm going to sneak in and surprise them. Do you know how to drive?"

"Sort of." One of her foster parents had taught her the basics.

"Great. You'll be our getaway driver. Here are the keys. Get in the driver's seat and wait. We might need to get away fast."

"All right," Jaxon said. She had no intention of following orders but knew they had no time for another argument. "Good luck."

Vivian nodded and loped off down the street. Four little girls playing a game with pebbles in one of the empty lots stared at Vivian curiously. Jaxon figured that foreign women didn't go jogging in their neighborhood very often. When the girls noticed Jaxon hanging out by the Land Rover, they came over.

They made a half circle around her and stared up with big, curious brown eyes. All wore threadbare but clean djellabas and headscarves. Their little brown bare feet were powdered with pale sand.

One nudged another. The one who got nudged, who looked about eight, stepped forward and asked something in Arabic.

Jaxon grinned at her. "Sorry, I'm trying to learn Arabic, but I don't even know enough to know what you asked, let alone answer you."

This brought forth a chorus of giggles.

"Hello, what country?" the one in front recited in heavily accented English.

"America," Jaxon said, giving Vivian a nervous look as she disappeared around the corner. "Look, I don't have time for a language exchange right now. I'm about to risk my life trying to save my people here."

She locked the Land Rover, pocketed the keys, and hustled down the street. To her dismay, the little girls followed her.

Jaxon turned. They stopped. "Look, I can't have you tagging along. Get going."

She motioned for them to leave. All that earned her was more giggles. They imitated her motion and giggled some more.

"No, I'm serious, get going!"

"Geeet goeeinggg!" the girls imitated.

Jaxon rolled her eyes. Normally this would be funny and cute, but this was not a normal day.

Actually risking my life has become way too normal lately, Jaxon thought.

"Move!" she shouted, kicking sand at them.

They stared at her, confused. Irritated, she picked up a pebble and threw it at them, taking care not to hit them.

"I said move!"

Two ran off. One burst into tears. The fourth gave her the finger.

"You watch too many American films, kid," Jaxon told her and ran after Vivian. While she felt bad about bullying a group of little girls, at least they weren't following her into a gunfight anymore.

Jaxon rounded the corner just in time to hear the first explosion.

The first thing she saw was a large concrete block of a house with shuttered windows. A muscular man lay on the ground next to the front door. It lay open, and smoke issued from it.

"You sure know how to make an entrance, Vivian!" Jaxon said with a laugh.

She felt the old thrill again, the same thrill she had felt when she and Brett Lawson had gone hunting criminals in the worst neighborhoods of Los Angeles. The thrill of purposely going into danger.

Jaxon picked up speed until she was beating the average Olympic sprinter. Not enough to win the gold, perhaps. She needed some practice.

The thought amused her so much she almost overshot the house. She had to dig in her heels, plowing a pair of deep furrows in the dirt road, in order to stop in time. A nervous face stared at her from an open doorway across the street. The door quickly slammed shut.

Jaxon hurried past the unconscious body of the sentry and to the front door, took a quick peek inside to make sure no one was waiting to shoot her, and entered.

Like with most houses in this region, the first room was a large sitting room for guests and socializing. Vivian's sense of socializing was to toss a stun grenade inside. Two men who looked Russian lay on the thick carpet, out cold. One had his head resting on one of the many pillows that lined the edges of the room. If it weren't for the smoke hanging in the room and their rumpled clothing, they would have looked like they were taking a nap. Gunfire echoed down the hallway leading off into the rest of the house.

Jaxon peeked around the corner and saw Vivian at the end of the hallway, firing into a room at someone Jaxon couldn't see. The mercenary ducked back as bullets pockmarked the concrete wall. She reached into her pocket, pulled out another stun grenade, and tossed it into the room.

A flash and a deafening boom. Vivian peeked around the corner. Jaxon moved to join her.

Just then a doorway between her and the mercenary opened, and a muscular man gripping a pistol jumped out and aimed at the back of Vivian's head. Jaxon's ears rang from the explosion of the stun grenade, and no doubt Vivian's did too, because she didn't turn at the sound of the Russian's approach.

Jaxon rushed down the hallway and slammed into him. Even though the man was twice her size, he flew forward as if he weighed no more than a pillow. His arms gyrated as he tried to regain his balance, his gun firing harmlessly into the ceiling, and he landed hard at Vivian's feet, knocking himself out on the concrete floor.

The mercenary turned in surprise. She gave Jaxon a thumbs-up. Words were pointless, thanks to the ringing in their ears.

Vivian motioned for her to leave, the same motion Jaxon had tried on the little girls a couple of minutes before. Jaxon was tempted to give the same response. Instead she just shook her head.

This was no place for an argument. Vivian peeked around the corner. When no shots came, Jaxon did too. Another man, this one with an AK-47 assault rifle, lay stunned on the floor. A door lay open at the opposite end of the room. They ran for it.

Halfway across the room, a man popped out from the other side of the doorway and aimed a pistol. Jaxon's hand whipped out, grabbed a chair she was passing, and flung it at the gunman.

It missed, splintering against the doorframe, but it came close enough to make him duck back around the corner.

Vivian shoved her aside and got next to the doorway. She thrust her arm around the corner and took several unaimed shots, poked her head around the corner, and then eased into the doorway.

The man lay dead just on the other side. Three

bullets had found him, two in the chest and one in the face. Jaxon retched and looked away. Suddenly this wasn't so much fun anymore. That could have been her. That could have been Vivian. It was bad enough it was him.

She dared another glance at the dead Russian, unable to look away. His face bore a look of surprise, like it had never occurred to him that it could end this way. Jaxon wondered if he had family back in Russia somewhere. Of course he did. Most people weren't orphans like her. Most people had family in their lives. Loved ones. A pool of blood spread out on the concrete floor around him. Its edge reached Jaxon's shoe. She shuddered and pulled away.

I helped do that to him, she realized. *These people kidnapped my boyfriend and ended up making me an accessory to murder.*

Why couldn't people just leave the Atlanteans alone? Why have all this killing in the first place?

Jaxon stood stunned for a moment. It took her several seconds to snap out of it, and when she did, she discovered that Vivian had disappeared.

A roar of gunfire from another room told her where she had gone. Jaxon hurried in that direction, eager to get away from the body in the hall. She came to another doorway, paused, and peeked around.

It looked like a computer lab. Vivian huddled behind an upturned table next to Yuhle and Otto and exchanged fire with a couple of Russians hiding behind a doorway on the opposite side of the room. Several shattered computers lay strewn on the floor between them. The Russians had the better cover— concrete walls instead of a thick wooden table, and their steady fire kept her friends' heads down. Bullets chewed up the table.

Jaxon ducked back into the hallway, her stomach twisting when she saw she had left bloody footprints on the floor, and went to a little side table that sat against one wall with a vase stuffed with plastic flowers. She grabbed both and got back into the fight.

First she tossed the vase, which smashed against the doorjamb the Russians hid behind. It made them flinch, giving Vivian enough time to return fire.

The Russians recovered the next instant. One shot at Vivian, forcing her to drop to the floor once more, and the other aimed at Jaxon.

Using her superhuman speed, she easily ducked behind the doorway before he even got to fire. The bullet planted itself harmlessly in the far wall.

Without exposing herself, she tossed the side table at them. She could barely hear it crash over the ringing in her ears.

She peeked around the corner and had to duck back the next instant to avoid getting her head blown off. She'd missed again.

Then she heard a scream and a pair of loud thuds.

"What the—" Vivian shouted and cut off.

Jaxon looked around the corner again and couldn't believe her eyes.

Brett, her old friend from Los Angeles, stood in the far doorway, holding the crumpled forms of the two Russians, one in each fist. He looked blankly around the room. Vivian was crouched behind the table, her gun visible and pointing at him, but Brett didn't seem to notice her. In fact, he didn't seem to notice much of anything.

Jaxon blinked. That couldn't be Brett. He'd been killed by that gang back when they had been out hunting criminals. Brett was dead.

And yet there he stood.

"Brett!" she called.

"You know that kid?" Vivian asked.

Jaxon didn't get to answer, because at the sound of Jaxon's voice, Brett whipped around, saw her, and ran straight for her.

"How is this possible? How did you get here?" she asked, opening her arms to embrace him.

Instead of a hug, she got a punch in the stomach that sent her ten feet down the hall to land hard on her backside.

Jaxon's head reeled. How could he have hit her so hard? And why had he hit her? For abandoning him to those thugs? She hadn't meant to!

"Brett, wait, I—"

Brett picked her up by the collar with one hand and punched her with the other. Her vision exploded in a supernova of light, and she almost passed out. Dimly she saw his fist pull back for another punch. She whipped both hands out and grasped it.

Her friend struggled to free himself and almost succeeded. How could he have grown so strong? He looked the same.

No, now that her vision was clearing, she could see that he didn't look the same. Where once he had had a confident, sly look and kind of a dumb optimism, now his face was almost blank. It was like he was drugged or sleepwalking or something. He looked completely out of it.

Not so out of it that he couldn't fight. He let go of her, wrenched his hand free, and tried to strangle her. Jaxon batted his grasping hands away and backed off.

"What's wrong with you? Brett, it's me!"

Gunfire was going off in the other room again, but she didn't have time to pay it any attention. Brett lunged for her again.

Too fast. He shot in like lightning, and Jaxon, not expecting such a quick attack, found herself getting picked up and thrown against a wall. She slammed into the bare concrete and landed with a loud thud on the floor.

It would have broken the bones of a normal person, but Jaxon was no normal person.

Neither was Brett. Not anymore.

Jaxon rolled away just before Brett stomped on her head.

She leapt to her feet and ran back a few steps, trying to get some distance between her and the maniac that had once been her friend.

Brett didn't give her that chance. He came right after her.

He swung at her with a fist that she now knew could hurt her. She blocked it at the last moment and then had to back off and block the next attack.

And again. And again. He came at her with relentless determination and inhuman speed and strength. Jaxon didn't have time to wonder how this was all possible. It was all she could do to stay alive.

Terror gripped her heart to see that soulless look in his eyes. She would have preferred anything else. Even murderous rage would have been better, but he tried to take her life with the blank, thoughtless gaze of a shark.

Jaxon finally saw an opening and struck out with a right hook that caught Brett in the ribs. It should have broken them and put him on the floor for the next ten minutes, but instead he merely grunted and lashed out at her again as the gunfire in the other room rose to a crescendo.

She blocked it with an inch to spare and took another step back. Okay, this couldn't be Brett, and yet it was. It looked just like him. But how could he be here in Timbuktu, and how could he be fighting like this?

Jaxon barely had time for the thought in between dodging, blocking, and ducking his attacks. Brett had always bragged about his martial arts training, and he had actually been pretty good, but now he was ten times as fast and twenty times as strong as before.

Another punch got through, sending Jaxon staggering back several feet. Brett dove in for the kill, and she landed a front kick in the dead center of his chest. This time she didn't hold back on her strength. Instinct didn't let her. She kicked with enough force to shatter the sternum and drive its splinters into his heart. For a second, her own heart did a flip-flop at the realization of what she had done.

A moment later, her heart turned to ice. What should have been a fatal blow only stopped him in his tracks. The next instant, she was lifted off her feet, flipped over Brett's shoulder, and thrown back toward the room from which he had come.

She landed hard on the floor and rolled a couple of yards, ending up at Grunt and Vivian's feet.

Grunt? How did he get here?

He looked pale and was covered in bloody bandages, and yet he gripped an AK-47 with the same determination as his old comrade-in-arms.

Grunt and Vivian opened fire on Brett.

Jaxon screamed. Both let loose with their assault rifles on full auto, hitting Brett with a hailstorm of bullets. Her old friend staggered backward, his chest tearing apart, his shirt and pants instantly turning red, and then he stopped, held his ground, and, as Jaxon looked on in terror, actually stomped forward against the fusillade of bullets like a man leaning against a hard wind.

He made it three whole steps before he crumpled and fell.

CHAPTER 15

AUGUST 15, 2016, TIMBUKTU
4:30 P.M.

Otto sat in the back of the Land Rover as it sped through the last of the dusty lanes on the edge of town and onto a flat open track shooting straight out into the desert. Vivian was at the wheel, and she slammed on the gas, picking up speed. Grunt lay sprawled in the passenger's seat, looking half dead, while Otto, Yuhle, and Jaxon were stuffed into the back seat. Dr. Yamazaki was with the other Land Rover somewhere and had called to set up a rendezvous.

Otto wasn't sure where or when they'd meet, and he couldn't worry about that now. At the moment, Jaxon lay curled up on his lap sobbing.

"What happened? What happened?" she kept crying out.

"I have no idea, honey," Vivian said. "Who was that kid?"

"Brett," Jaxon said between sobs.

Brett. Now Otto remembered. She had mentioned him. Some kid at her school when she had been adopted by Isadore Grant. Isadore had been at the house too, showing up out of nowhere with Brett before Grunt appeared a minute later, grabbed an AK-47 off a body, and started firing at her. By then, all the Russians were down except Dimitri and Nadya, who had disappeared, but the fight got even nastier than before. Otto couldn't believe he had gotten out of there in one piece. It was like an international convention of badasses.

Isadore had gotten away in one piece too, right after Brett got killed.

"Brett!" Jaxon wailed.

Otto stroked her shoulder, feeling at a loss. Why would an old schoolmate mean so much to her? And why in the world would he show up here? Then a third question came to his mind. It bubbled up his throat and came out before he could stop it.

"Was Brett spying on you all along for Isadore? Is that why they were together?"

"No!" Jaxon wailed. "He got killed by a gang in LA."

"Obviously not," Grunt said from the front seat. His voice sounded weak. Otto looked at him nervously.

"He couldn't have been in on it," Jaxon whispered.

Vivian looked at her in the rearview mirror. "He was beating you. I saw. How?"

Jaxon shook her head, getting Otto's jeans wet with her tears.

"He had all the characteristics of an Atlantean," Dr. Yuhle said, squinting at them. His glasses had been broken in the fight.

"He didn't look like an Atlantean," Otto said.

"No," Yuhle replied. "But he sure moved like one."

"He wasn't that fast and strong before, was he?" Otto asked. It seemed like a stupid question, but he had to ask.

Jaxon shook her head again, convulsing with

sobs. Her grief had taken her beyond speech. Otto felt a spike of jealousy. Just who was this guy to her?

He tried to ignore the emotion. It wasn't worthy of him. The guy had just been killed, after all. But still—just who was this guy to her?

"Are we almost at the rendezvous?" Grunt asked faintly. Otto could barely hear him.

"Hang in there, buddy," Vivian said. She held up her hand for a high five. Grunt didn't respond. After a moment's hesitation, she let her hand fall.

"Just what happened to you, anyway?" Otto asked.

"Met some trouble up in Marrakech in the shape of identical twins swinging straight razors. That trouble's coming this way."

Great, Otto thought. *Just what we need—more trouble.*

"Are you okay?" Otto asked. *Another stupid question.*

Grunt turned in his seat, his head lolling to the side.

"You're a good kid, Otto. Don't forget that," the mercenary said.

Otto glanced at Yuhle and found the geneticist looking right at him. Or at least trying to. He squinted too much to make eye contact, but his expression was unmistakable.

To avoid that expression, Otto turned back to Grunt.

"This is no time for dramatic dying speeches," he told the mercenary.

"But I am dying, pyro."

"Not if I can help it," Vivian said, gripping the wheel. "We're almost to Yamazaki."

Jaxon jerked up in the seat. Otto pulled back, startled.

"Does she have the water? We could go back and heal Brett!" she shouted.

Vivian turned and looked her right in the eye. Somehow she kept the Land Rover moving on a straight track. Not that it mattered out here. The land was so barren that there was nothing to hit.

"Now listen here, honey. I know you're all torn up about your friend, but Brett's dead. Grunt is only dying. The water can help Grunt but not your friend."

"You don't know that!" Jaxon cried. "We've never tried it on a dead person before."

"Nothing can raise the dead, honey," Vivian said.

Yuhle pressed his fingertip against the bridge of

his nose as if to adjust a set of glasses he no longer wore and said, "Well, theoretically—"

"Shut up, pencil neck," Vivian snapped.

Yuhle shut up.

"We should try!" Jaxon said.

"And let Grunt die?" Vivian said, finally looking back at the road.

Silence. Finally, Jaxon spoke again.

"Maybe there's enough to heal both of them," she said. She sounded like she was trying to convince herself.

The other Land Rover appeared in the distance, coming toward them at an angle along a different dirt track. Within a minute, the two vehicles screeched to a halt in front of each other. Vivian leapt out and sprinted over to Dr. Yamazaki, who stepped out holding the plastic bottle containing the last of the healing water.

Jaxon got out of the Land Rover and ran toward them.

"No, wait! We need to save it for Brett!"

"Who?" Dr. Yamazaki asked.

Otto caught up to his girlfriend and grabbed her by the shoulders.

"Grunt needs it. He'll die!"

Jaxon shook him off with enough strength that Otto almost fell.

"Go away. We need to go back and help him."

"Listen," Otto said. "We don't know the water will help a dead person." Jaxon sobbed when he said this, but he went on. She had to see reason. "Besides, if we go back there, we'll run into the Russians or Isadore or the cops, maybe all three. We can't risk another firefight. What if another of us gets hurt? We don't have any way to heal them."

Jaxon paused. Otto could see her hope for Brett and the cold, hard facts of his words struggling for dominance in her mind. Vivian took the water bottle and hurried back to Grunt. Jaxon watched her go and then sank slowly to the ground, her body convulsed with sobs. Otto moved to comfort her.

Vivian opened the plastic bottle and carefully tipped back Grunt's head. He was barely conscious now, and Vivian had to feed him like a baby. Otto watched in fascination as the color began to come back to the mercenary's face. His eyes opened, and he sat up straighter in his seat. He hadn't even finished the bottle yet. By the time he drained it a few seconds later, he was smiling.

Forgetting Jaxon for a moment, Otto hurried over to his friend.

"You okay?" he asked.

Grunt grinned at him. "You can't keep a bad man down."

"Since when have you been bad?" Otto asked with a laugh.

"I do my best, pyro," Grunt said. Otto flushed with delight to hear him sound so healthy, even if he was calling him "pyro."

Grunt gave Vivian a high five and stepped out of the Land Rover. For some reason he lifted his face to the sun a moment and smiled. Then he took his shirt off. He peeled off his bandages one by one, only to find his cuts had healed.

"Two crazies slashed me with straight razors," he muttered. "Hey, look at this."

He held up one of the bandages. Stuck on the inside were a bunch of bits of thread.

Dr. Yuhle leaned in close to them, squinting. "Interesting. Your skin pushed out the stitches as it healed."

Grunt pointed to the last bandage, one on his lower left side.

"One of the guys cut me deep in the gut. Caused lots of internal bleeding. That's what almost killed me. A contact got me a black-market surgeon to patch me up, but I sprang a leak coming down here. You think the water healed that too?"

"It healed my severed spine," Dr. Yuhle said. "That's a far more serious injury."

Grunt shrugged. "Only one way to find out."

"Careful," Vivian said.

Slowly Grunt peeled off the last bandage. Otto realized he was holding his breath.

Beneath the bandage, his skin didn't even bear a mark.

"Thank God!" Otto cried and threw his arms around him. Suddenly he found he was crying. He tried to stop but couldn't.

"Whoa, hey! Easy there, pyro." Grunt stood there stiffly, obviously not knowing what to do. Eventually he returned the hug. "It's all right now, buddy."

After a minute, Otto detached himself and wiped his eyes, somewhat embarrassed by his outburst.

"So how did the Russians get the two of you, anyway?" Grunt asked.

Otto looked at Yuhle. The scientist paused a moment and then said, "Jumped us in our rooms. There was nothing we could do."

"Well, we're all together now, and we're not splitting up again," Grunt said. "We left Edward behind, and he ended up getting killed by Isadore."

Everyone bowed their heads to hear the news they had been dreading.

"And you two almost got killed when we split up the next time," Grunt went on, "not to mention yours truly."

"We won't make the same mistake again," Vivian said.

Otto saw Jaxon still sniffling and sitting on the ground. He moved back to her. Guilt over Nadya and jealousy about Brett mingled in his mind. Sitting down next to her, he rubbed her back and tried to think of something to say but couldn't come up with anything that didn't sound stupid. He had never had to deal with much death before, just old people. Brett looked like he had been their age.

"Oh, I almost forgot!" Yuhle said, and handed a vial of red liquid to Dr. Yamazaki. "We need to get this into the cooler for later analysis."

Jaxon perked up. "What is that?"

The two scientists moved to Yamazaki's Land Rover, where they had a small electric-powered cooler as part of their mobile lab.

"What is that?" Jaxon asked again, standing up.

Yuhle looked embarrassed. "It's, um, a blood sample."

"From Brett?" Jaxon demanded.

"Yes, sorry, but we have to know how he got such strength and speed."

Jaxon stormed over to him. "You drained his blood right after he was shot? What are you, a vampire?"

Yuhle quickly put the sample in the cooler. Jaxon pushed him and Yamazaki to one side.

"Let me have that!" she shouted.

Otto rushed over to her. "Easy there!"

"I'm going to give it a decent burial," she growled.

Otto hesitated. His girlfriend, if she still was his girlfriend, could break him in half, and she wasn't exactly in a good mood right now.

Jaxon opened the cooler and pulled out the vial. Otto raised his hands in a calming gesture.

"Look, I know you're all torn up about your friend." *Or boyfriend,* Otto added silently. "But you saw how he fought. Isadore or General Meade did something to him. We have to find out what."

"Honey, I've never seen someone take that many bullets before falling," Vivian said. "It wasn't natural."

"I probably could," Jaxon said, staring at the vial.

Otto blinked. Yeah, she probably could. "Do you think maybe they injected him with Atlantean blood or something?"

"Theoretically that's possible," Dr. Yuhle said. "Although the actual process would probably not be so straightforward. Meade may be trying to replicate Atlantean powers in regular people. That's why we need to analyze that sample."

Jaxon kept staring at the vial. After a minute, she wiped away her tears, put the vial back in the cooler, and walked off into the desert.

"We need to get out of here, get farther away from town," Grunt said.

"Give her some time," Otto whispered.

"The cops will be looking for us," Grunt said.

"Give her some time," Otto repeated, watching Jaxon's distant figure recede into the glaring wasteland of the Sahara.

CHAPTER 16

AUGUST 17, 2016, A VILLAGE ON THE
HIGHWAY 25 MILES EAST OF TIMBUKTU
NOON

Jaxon had never felt so much pain in her entire life.

It had been two days since the fight, two days since Brett had come back from the dead only to be taken from her a second time. Two days of misery.

All the guilt of his disappearance and supposed death back in Los Angeles came back at her tenfold. This time it really was her fault. She still couldn't make sense of it. He had attacked her, and she'd had to defend herself. Vivian and Grunt had shot him to save her. They had all done what they had needed to do. But she couldn't get around the fact that if she hadn't followed Vivian into that Russian hideout, Brett might be still alive today.

The Atlantis Allegiance had spent the past two days camping in a remote part of the desert. Jaxon had lain in her tent, hardly speaking with anyone. Otto had been kind, supportive, but what could he do to take this pain away? The others had kept their distance. She couldn't even look at the mercenaries, not after what they had done. The scientists had been busy in their little lab.

They'd gotten their results that morning.

"The findings are quite clear," Yuhle said, his face so close to his laptop that his nose almost touched the screen. He'd broken his last pair of glasses in the fight. "Brett's blood shows Atlantean traits. He has normal DNA, but all other factors are well within Atlantean parameters. He was a human–Atlantean hybrid."

Jaxon felt ill. General Meade had turned her friend into a lab rat.

"How?" Otto asked.

The geneticists shrugged.

"A very advanced technique," Yamazaki said.

"We don't have the resources to even begin to analyze it."

"He's creating an army, isn't he?" Otto said. "He wants an army of Atlanteans."

"Damn," Grunt muttered. "A regiment of those could raise some serious hell."

"This is what we feared all along," Vivian said. "Meade has gone completely rogue. I don't think he's doing this for the Pentagon or anyone up the chain of command. I think he's doing it for himself."

"That's certainly the impression we got while we worked for him," Dr. Yamazaki said. "That's why we left and formed the Atlantis Allegiance in the first place." She sighed and went on. "I guess all this time, I was hoping we were wrong."

Jaxon pulled herself out of her black thoughts long enough to ask, "Why would he do this?"

Everyone paused and looked at each other.

"A coup?" Grunt suggested.

"What? You mean like take over the United States?" Jaxon said.

The mercenary shrugged. "It's the only explanation I can think of. Why else would he want a private army?"

"The American people will never stand for it!" Otto said.

"How could they resist, if Meade's followers look like normal people but fight like superheroes?" Vivian said. "They won't know who the enemy is. Did you see the blank look on Brett's face? He was like a zombie."

Vivian visibly tensed as she realized she had said the wrong thing. She stole a guilty glance at Jaxon, who turned away.

"We need to get in contact with the Atlantean community back in Timbuktu and warn them," Jaxon said.

Otto shook his head. "We can't go back there. It's too risky."

Jaxon sighed. He was right. As much as she wanted to be comforted by her people right now, as much as she'd like to sit in the griot's front room and be surrounded by faces like hers, their enemies would be waiting for her back there.

"We don't have to," Jaxon said. "We just need to get to a place where we can get a signal and I can call them."

"Where?" Otto asked.

"There's that highway that runs just north of the River Niger," Jaxon said, pulling out a map of the region. "See how there's a bunch of villages along it? We can go to one of them."

And so they did. With Dr. Yamazaki driving, Vivian and Jaxon drove into a little village on the highway about twenty-five miles east of Timbuktu. The rest of the team stayed in the desert just beyond sight of the town. While they all remembered Grunt's warning about splitting up, they needed to be as inconspicuous as possible. The two Land Rovers stayed in constant contact via a pair of powerful walkie-talkies, which had a range of a couple of miles.

The village was a cluster of maybe two hundred adobe and concrete buildings with a couple of little mosques and not much else. Even the mosques, usually so beautiful in this region, having been made of sculpted adobe with towering minarets, were in this place ugly concrete blocks with a little tower where tinny loud-speakers called the faithful to prayer. It seemed, as Jaxon looked at the mechanics' shops and tire stores and cafés, that this place existed entirely for serving the truckers and buses going along the highway. There was certainly no agriculture. This village and the highway itself ran through the desert well north of the irrigated section fed by the river. The cracked and potholed streets were covered with a fine layer of sand. In this part of the world, farmland was too valuable to build on.

They didn't get a decent signal until they were near the center of town. In fact, they could see the mobile phone tower, a rusty metal contraption stuck on top of a three-story concrete building that looked like a block of offices. Dr. Yamazaki parked by a busy square nearby.

"Make your calls and let's get out of here, honey," Vivian said, looking around nervously.

Jaxon opened the door.

"What are you doing?" Vivian asked.

"Getting some privacy," Jaxon snapped. She knew it was unfair to use that tone on her friend, who was only being careful, but she couldn't get the image of Vivian shooting Brett out of her head.

She closed the door behind her. Dr. Yamazaki rolled down her window.

"It would be safer if you made the call from inside."

"I'll just be a minute," Jaxon replied, taking out her cell phone and walking away.

"Uh-oh, there's a cop car down the street," Vivian called to her. "They're coming this way."

Jaxon turned back toward the Land Rover.

"Don't do that, honey. I don't want them to spot you too. Walk past like you don't know us. They might be on the watch for us. We'll circle around and pick you up in a minute."

"All right," Jaxon replied, her heart beating fast.

Dr. Yamazaki drove off at a slow speed so as not to look suspicious. Jaxon glanced at the police vehicle out of the corner of her eye. It was a blue pickup truck with a couple of Kalashnikov-toting cops sitting in the back and two more in the cab. They looked curiously at the Land Rover but didn't seem to notice Jaxon at all.

Jaxon bit her lip. Best not to push her luck. She was wearing that headscarf Otto had given her, making her look more like a local, but she still wore Western-style clothing. As casually as she could, holding the phone to her ear as if she were talking, she tried to merge with the pedestrians crossing to and fro on the square. She made for the nearest street, so she could get around the corner and out of sight.

A few passersby stared at her, giving her the usual confused look the locals did when they saw one of the People of the Sea who didn't dress like she was from Africa. She cursed herself for not getting proper clothes when she'd had the chance in Timbuktu.

At least they didn't try to talk with her since she

had the phone up to her ear. And Jaxon thanked her luck that school was in session. That kept her from attracting a little crowd of children pestering her with questions. The cops would definitely notice that.

Jaxon turned a little, putting her finger in her ear as if she was having trouble hearing the imaginary person on the phone. That gave her a chance to peek at the Land Rover, which was just moving out of sight.

The police vehicle was following. In a heart-stopping moment, she clearly saw the driver pick up the mic for the truck's radio and start talking.

Jaxon got out of the square and hurried down a street and through a little market. Village women from the nearby river had come to sell produce. A little row of them sat in the meager shade of a row of tumbledown concrete buildings while they haggled with customers over the price of a variety of vegetables, grain, and baked bread.

Jaxon stopped and dialed Salif's number.

"Jaxon? Where are you?" he asked when he picked up. He sounded worried.

"We had some trouble with the Russians, and then some American agents too," Jaxon said. "We saved Yuhle and Otto, though."

"Are you all right?"

"Yes," she lied. She didn't feel all right and knew she wouldn't for a long time.

"Well, you certainly left a big mess behind you," Salif growled.

"What?"

"The police have been here. They know that your group of foreigners were fighting the other group of foreigners, and they want to know why. Did you think the police never took note of you? And now that you have run away, they are asking all the People of the Sea questions. They have discovered how we brought the refugees from Ras el Ma, and now they are suspicious of our intentions. Jaxon, they might send them back over the border!"

"What? They can't do that! They'll be taken to that camp."

"The police do not know about this. All they see is a group of Americans meddling with their politics and then getting into a gunfight with a group of Russians. They say the house was full of bodies. The Russian ambassador is coming up from Bamako!"

"Oh no, this is terrible. I am so sorry."

"Sorry isn't good enough," Salif said, his anger audible through the crackly connection. "I warned you to be careful. I warned you there might be trouble, and now we have the government thinking we are in league with a violent foreign group. This is the very same thing the Mauritanian government said about our people before they put them in a prison camp. Do you want us sent away too?"

"Salif, you know that was never my intention."

"Never mind your intention. You have brought disaster down on all of our heads! I tell you to be careful, I tell you not to bring attention to yourself, and you get in gunfights?"

"We didn't have a choice about that."

"And we may not have a choice to remain here."

Salif hung up.

Jaxon looked around. People had heard her speaking in English, and she had attracted some attention. A man approached her with a welcoming smile. Jaxon pretended she didn't notice him and walked quickly away. Her phone rang. The screen said it was Vivian.

"You okay?" Jaxon asked.

"If by okay you mean driving at eighty miles an hour through the desert with the cops hot on our tail, then yes, we're okay."

She could hear thuds and bangs in the background as the Land Rover darted over rough terrain.

The connection began to get crackly as they sped farther away from the cell phone tower.

"Oh no!" Jaxon cried. "Can you hear me?"

"What? Don't worry. Yamazaki is an ace driver —" Vivian said something else that got lost in the static—"She lost those last cops, and she'll lose these. You sit tight, and we'll get back to you somehow. Go to—"

The connection cut off.

Jaxon paused in the middle of the street, unsure what to do. A donkey brushed by her. A couple of women tried to address her in Arabic, and she nodded and walked off.

I'm attracting too much attention.

She walked for a time and spotted a women's clothing shop. While most women preferred to make their own clothes in Mali, one could buy cheap ready-made clothes. Jaxon hurried in to buy some loose robes that would make her look more like a local.

That turned out to be a big mistake.

"Welcome to my country!" said the teenaged daughter of the storeowner. "I took English in school. It is so good to be able to practice. Come, have some tea."

Getting stuck for a couple of hours of African hospitality was not what Jaxon had in mind.

At least tea was in a back room, away from the prying eyes of the street. As Jaxon chatted with the girl, who was about her age, and through her talked with the girl's mother, Jaxon wondered how much word was getting around that a foreigner who looked like one of the People of the Sea had come shopping for clothes. She figured in a small town like this, word traveled fast, but with it being right on the country's major highway, maybe they were a bit more used to foreigners.

She hoped.

One glass of tea turned into two, and the shop-keepers chattered on and on, asking her endless questions about life in the United States. She made up a story about being a tourist visiting Timbuktu and having come out here to see what a smaller town looked like. They found that hilarious. "Not even we want to live here, and you come all the way from America to visit? Timbuktu is much more interesting." After the third glass of tea and now feeling fully sugared up, Jaxon excused herself a couple of times to try and call Vivian, but she didn't pick up. She tried Otto, too, in the other Land Rover, but he was out of range too.

Finally she got around to business and managed to buy a loose robe that made her look more like a local. She also bought a colorful fabric bag to put her old Western clothes in.

"You take the bus back to Timbuktu?" the daughter asked.

"Um, yeah," Jaxon said to sound convincing.

"It stops on the next square. It should come soon, God willing."

"Thanks!"

Jaxon headed that way to make her story of being a tourist look believable. The square lay close to the highway, visible through a gap in the buildings. Several trucks rumbled by. The plaza itself had several buses and minibuses parked in the center with the drivers shouting out their destinations.

She turned away from the noise, pulled out her phone, and tried calling the other members of the Atlantis Allegiance. Still no luck. Then she dialed Hawa Ndiaye's number.

"Jaxon!" the Atlantean schoolteacher cried when she picked up. "Are you safe?"

"Um, yeah," Jaxon replied, not sure that she was. As she answered, she saw a police pickup truck pass slowly through the square. She didn't think it was the same one that had gone off to chase Vivian and

Yamazaki, but she couldn't be sure. "What's going on back there?"

Hawa Ndiaye's voice dropped to a frightened whisper. "The police came and asked me about you. They knew we spent time together. There are so few foreigners here that everyone knew your movements. Now they are saying you are a spy! They took my grandfather to the police station!"

Jaxon's hands trembled at the thought of that kindly old storyteller and historian being dragged off to be questioned.

The police truck drove up the street Jaxon stood on. She turned her back on it, ready to run if she got spotted.

She let out a sigh of relief when the police drove past without slowing.

Her friend was still talking. "They are questioning everybody. They are going house to house. We haven't had shooting in the street since Al-Qaeda got kicked out. Everyone is blaming our community for bringing war back to Timbuktu."

Jaxon winced. Her arrival had brought disaster to the very people she was trying to protect.

"What can I do?" Jaxon asked.

"I don't know. Nothing. If the police see you here, they will arrest you."

If the police see me here, they'll arrest me just as quickly, Jaxon thought, taking a nervous look around.

The police truck passed by again. It drove slowly, the men inside studying the crowd, obviously looking for someone.

Looking for her.

Jaxon stepped into a doorway, ignoring someone nearby staring at the locally dressed woman speaking English, and asked, "Did they capture Nadya and Dimitri?"

"No. The police are looking for them, but I think they are gone. It is the Russian ambassador I am worried about. He will be angry that some of his people have been killed, and he will want the government to punish us."

Jaxon ground her teeth. All she wanted was to find her place in the world, and now she was ending up a burden to her people. Before she could think of something to say, Hawa Ndiaye went on.

"There are some more strangers here."

"Oh no, now what?" Jaxon sighed. The last thing they needed was even more trouble.

"I don't know for sure. They are Atlanteans, or at least they look like the People of the Sea. They are strange, though. They wear local clothes but do not act like locals. From what I hear, only one of them speaks Arabic and speaks it like a foreigner. The rest do not talk to anyone."

"Wait, foreigners who are Atlanteans? Where are they from? What are they doing there?"

"I don't know. They haven't contacted any of us. They were seen in the market asking questions. They visited the manuscript museum as well. I don't know more."

Jaxon dared a look out of the doorway. The police truck had stopped at an intersection, and one of the officers had stepped out to speak with a man leading a camel. The man pointed back in the direction Jaxon had come. Back in the direction of the clothing shop.

Great, Jaxon thought. *I'm going to get even more people in trouble.*

I need to watch it, or I'll be next.

"Look, Hawa, I need to go. I'll talk to you soon."

Before her friend could say more, Jaxon hung up. She waited until the police officer got back in the truck and drove off toward the clothing shop before she stepped out of the doorway. Now several people were staring, and she realized she had been behaving suspiciously.

She couldn't stay here. Her disguise had bought her some time, but sooner or later, they'd find her.

Jaxon headed for the square where the buses gathered. Dialing the Atlantis Allegiance one more time and still getting no answer, she hurried toward a cluster of rattling old buses. People piled on, jamming the insides, while some even climbed onto the roof. In front of each bus, a young man called out the destinations. Most meant nothing to her, but she saw one rusty heap packed with people with a man standing at the door shouting, "Timbuktu! Timbuktu!"

She went up to him and, not wanting to speak, handed over what she hoped was enough money. The young man said something back. Jaxon shrugged and held up the banknote. He said something else. Jaxon prayed this wasn't the start of a conversation. The driver took the money, gave her more change than she expected, and began calling out his destination again. Jaxon thanked her luck that he was too busy to speak with her.

Jaxon climbed aboard and found there was nowhere to sit. Every seat was taken up by at least one person, and everyone had a baby or a bag in their lap. The aisles were filled with people sitting on the floor. At the back was a huge pile of sacks. Some people sat on top of them, scrunched between the top of the sacks and the roof. Jaxon spotted a few places left back there, so she picked her way through the people crammed into the aisle, sometimes having to lift herself up on the seats and swing over people too crammed in to move out of the way.

Finally she made her way back to the sacks, which turned out to be filled with cheap sneakers imported from China, found a lumpy spot, and the bus roared off, headed back to the place that had nearly killed her a couple of days before.

This is insane, she told herself, and yet she couldn't keep away from Timbuktu. Even though every logical part of her mind begged her to get off at the next stop, she stayed in her place. She had messed up everything back in Timbuktu, and she had to set it right. She had spent a lifetime of leaving messes behind. Now it was time to grow up and take responsibility. Plus Hawa's mention of some foreign Atlanteans arriving in town had piqued her curiosity. Who could they be? She had to find out.

It sure helped that she couldn't stay in the town she had just left. It wasn't safe. In fact, no place was safe for her anymore.

And if she was going to be in danger, she might as well be in danger someplace where she could be useful.

CHAPTER 17

AUGUST 17, 2016, TIMBUKTU
2:30 P.M.

By the time the bus pulled into the main square of Timbuktu under the shadow of the great adobe mosque with its towering minarets and wooden support beams sticking out of the walls like the quills of a hedgehog, Jaxon swore she would never take public transport in Mali ever again. The bus had taken more than an hour to go twenty-five miles, stopping at every town, village, and roadside market on the way. No one got off, but plenty of people got on. It seemed like everyone was going to Timbuktu.

The few remaining spots on the sacks of Chinese sneakers soon filled up. But still the bus filled. A seemingly endless influx of people and luggage got crammed into an ever-smaller space. One man even brought a chicken coop aboard. Jaxon ended up with someone's toddler on her lap and squished against one of the windows by the press of bodies, the breeze from the open windows blowing sand and chicken feathers into her face.

Even with all the windows open, it soon grew oppressively hot. The toddler squalled with discomfort, and nothing Jaxon or her mother, crushed at her side, could do would calm her down.

And of course everyone almost immediately found out Jaxon was a foreigner. Soon a young man in Western clothing clambered over the mass of bodies, somehow found a place to sit nearby by inserting himself between two people who were able to move just enough for him to get one hip on the pile of shoes, introduced himself as a local university student, and started a long conversation with her. For the entire ride, he peppered her with all sorts of questions about who she was and why she was on a rattling old bus on a Malian highway.

She'd had a million of these conversations since

she'd come to Africa. It was simple curiosity on their part, but now it felt like a police cross-examination.

Because, in a way, it was. The police were searching for an American who looked like one of the People of the Sea. If they asked around enough, sooner or later they'd talk to one of the people on this bus and hear all about her.

She couldn't figure a way out of it, though, and kept up the conversation as the toddler wailed on her lap.

By the time the bus creaked to a halt on a broad square near the center of Timbuktu, Jaxon was almost faint from the heat and had a killer headache.

She didn't feel so bad that she didn't keep a sharp eye out as she stepped off the bus. A few cops stood not far off, smoking cigarettes and joking, their rifles slung casually over their shoulders. They didn't appear to be watching the passengers. Instead, they looked like routine security like most public places had in Mali.

That made her feel better. The cops were on the lookout for a pair of Land Rovers that had peeled out of Timbuktu, not for bus passengers coming into the city.

Wrapping her headscarf close about her face, she

walked to the nearest street leading away from the square. She resisted the urge to run. Now that she had made it back, she had to figure out what to do next. Go visit the Atlantean community? That could be risky with all eyes watching them. But she needed to get in touch with her friends and fix this mess somehow.

"Do you need help? Do you know where you are going?"

It was the university student from the bus, walking right next to her.

"No, I'm fine, thank you," she said, picking up a little speed.

"I can show you many interesting places in our city," he said, dogging her steps.

"No, thank you."

"Are you hungry? The marketplace has some wonderful—"

Jaxon straightened her spine and whirled on him. "You are being too forward. Would you like my husband to hear about this?"

The student stopped, eyes wide. He put up his hands as if to ward off a blow.

"So sorry! I didn't mean it that way. Good day."

The student hurried off.

Jaxon smiled. That was one thing she had

learned from Muslim women. Act regal and offended, and the guys usually backed off.

She glanced at the police. No, they hadn't witnessed that little blow-up.

She continued on her way.

But where should she go? Her Atlantean friends had warned her not to come back.

"Don't turn around, just keep walking in the direction you're walking," a low voice said behind her.

Jaxon whirled around. "Look, I told you—"

She cut off and immediately turned to face forward again, almost stumbling she did it so quickly. The person walking behind her wasn't the Malian student who had been speaking to her a minute ago. It was one of her own people, a man who looked to be in his thirties, wearing local clothing but speaking fluent English with a British accent.

"Who are you?" she whispered.

"A friend. Be careful. They're looking for you."

"Yeah, I noticed."

"You shouldn't have come back here," the man said, keeping his voice barely above a whisper.

"Who are you?" Jaxon asked again.

"We can talk once we get out of sight."

"Where can we go?"

"Down this road a little more. See that small shrine, the one with the domed roof? There's an alley to the right just beyond it. Go down that."

Jaxon's heart raced. This was one of the foreign Atlanteans her schoolteacher friend had told her about.

"Walk casually," he said, "as if you aren't with me. I am going to drop a little way behind before coming to join you."

Jaxon passed the shrine. It was one of the old tombs to medieval saints that attracted pilgrims from all over North Africa. It looked simple on the outside, just a square building with a low dome. The whole thing was painted green, the color of paradise. There were dozens of such shrines in Timbuktu, each with its own long story of the good deeds of its founder and the miracles that happened to the faithful who gathered there. She spotted the alley, a narrow space between the shrine and a madrasa, or religious school, right next to it. Through a small window high up in the wall, she could hear the rhythmic chanting of a group of young boys as they recited from the Koran.

As she entered the alley, she stumbled over a pile of bricks and some tools. Picking her way over the rubble, she moved further along. It was cooler here in the shade of the shrine. She noticed that large sections of it had been recently repaired. Half the roof and a big chunk of the wall had been replaced with new material.

"Smashed up by Al Qaeda in the Islamic Magreb," the stranger said as he joined her in the alley. He looked up at the new repairs and shook his head sadly. "This shrine is for a revered saint who lived nine hundred years ago. He was famous for teaching peace and for giving charity to orphans. A suitable place for us to have our little chat, isn't it?"

"Was he a Christian? Was that why the terrorists destroyed his shrine?" Jaxon asked.

"A Christian in Timbuktu? No, this has been a Muslim city for more than a thousand years. No, the saint was a Muslim like all the local saints, but the radical Islamists don't like shrines of any sort, especially if they honor a Muslim who preached peace."

"I'm a little more worried about my own government than I am about terrorists," Jaxon said.

The Englishman smiled. "My government isn't much better. But let's get down to business. I am Winston Chambers, an Atlantean like you."

"I can see that. I'm—"

"Jaxon Ares Anderson."

Jaxon blinked. "How did you know that?"

"We've been looking for you for quite some time. You're a hard girl to keep up with. I hope we've been of some small service to you and your friends."

"The team that saved Dr. Yamazaki from the hospital! That was you?"

"Please keep your voice down. Yes, that was us."

"One of you cured her stroke."

Winston bowed his head. "That was Rachel. She was our most talented healer."

Jaxon remembered Yamazaki had told her the entire team that had saved her had been gunned down by General Meade's agents. She bit her lip. More people getting hurt because of her.

Winston must have seen her expression, because he looked her in the eye and said in a firm voice, "Don't feel bad. They knew the risks, and we aren't doing all this just for you but for our entire people."

"So what's going on? And why follow me to Timbuktu?"

Winston paused, as if collecting his thoughts. "Because you're special. You're far more than an ordinary Atlantean."

"Why? Because of my powers? I can make plants grow, but that's nothing compared to curing a stroke."

"No, not because of your powers over plants but because of who your parents were."

The words hit her like a bolt of lightning. Her mind went blank, and she fell back until her back rested against the alley wall. If she had been standing out in the open, she would have fallen over.

"You knew my parents?" Her words came out in a hoarse croak.

"I knew them slightly. They were famous in our community back in London."

"London? I'm English?"

"No, a naturalized American. You were born in Portland, Oregon."

"Wait, my parents, are they here?"

"Please keep your voice down," Winston said, casting a nervous glance at the entrance to the alley. "Now stay calm. You're not going to like what I have to say."

Misery settled on Jaxon like a heavy blanket. She knew what was coming next. Of course, after all these years hoping to find her parents, she was going to meet someone who would tell her they were dead.

And the words came, relentless, cruel, and undeniable.

"Your parents fled England twenty years ago when a gang of organized criminals wanted to recruit

Atlanteans into their service. They had found out about us somehow, and while they weren't nearly as organized or sophisticated as General Meade's group, they were violent in the extreme. They threatened to kill your parents if they didn't comply. Your parents couldn't go to the police, because they knew they were being watched and this gang had connections with the police as well, so they fled to America. For a time they were safe, but the London gang had connections in America, and they tracked them down. By then you had been born. You were still an infant, and they knew the safest thing to do was to give you up for adoption."

"And my parents?"

Winston's face turned grim. "The criminals got them. I am terribly sorry."

"And my extended family?" Jaxon asked, feeling ill and leaning on the wall for support.

"We don't know about them."

"Why not?"

"Because we don't know your parents' real names."

"What? How come?"

Winston glanced at the opening of the alleyway again and lowered his voice as he continued. "Because they were the Keepers of the Texts. Like the griots here, they kept information about our heritage. And not just texts from the Middle Ages but actual original knowledge of our lost continent. The Keepers of the Texts is an office handed down from parents to children. Besides the individual power each Atlantean enjoys, they have an additional power, one vital to continuing our culture."

"What's that?"

"They can sense the old places, the places where our ancestors left knowledge. They are in tune with the powers that the old continent of Atlantis used to become the greatest civilization this world has ever seen."

Jaxon remembered that strange sensation she had had when they were dying of thirst in the desert, that certainty that they should make for a distant cluster of rocks when it lay in a different direction than the highway and their only reasonable chance of being saved. She had trusted her instincts, and she had found the wonderful healing water that had saved her and Vivian, and later Grunt.

But not Brett. She hadn't had enough to save Brett.

She pressed her hands against her eyes. This was all too much. Winston went on.

"Because of that, your parents, like the Keepers

before them, had to take care not to let outsiders find out their secrets. They lived a roaming life and used a series of false names. Not even their closest friends knew their real names. I never learned their real identities."

"So wait, you're telling me I don't even get to know my parents' names? How about my name?" Jaxon shook her head in disbelief. This was worse than not knowing anything about her past at all.

"When they gave you up, they wrote a single name on your blanket. The American Child Protective Services incorporated that into your legal name."

"Ares," Jaxon whispered. "It was Ares, wasn't it?"

Winston nodded.

She had always thought her middle name was strange. It was the name of the Greek god of war, a name she had never heard anyone else using, and a name that wasn't even a girl's name.

But it was a strong name, the name of a fighter. The name of a leader.

Jaxon felt a warmth spread through her chest. Her parents had loved her. Her parents had thought she had potential to do great things. None of the temporary foster parents she'd dealt with over the years had ever given her those two things.

She had something from them. It wasn't much, but it was something.

And that was a whole lot more than what she'd had before.

A shout in Arabic made her whirl around.

A policeman stood at the entrance to the alleyway, an AK-47 assault rifle in his hands. He stared at them and barked out a phrase that sounded like a question.

Jaxon tensed. This policeman had been ordered to keep an eye on the People of the Sea, and he'd found two of them hiding in an alleyway right next to a school. This did not look good.

The policeman shouted something again.

Winston put a finger to his lips. "Shhhh."

The policeman looked at him quizzically.

"It's all right," Winston said in a soothing voice and beckoned him to join them.

The policeman relaxed, his shoulders slumping and his hand falling away from the trigger of his weapon.

"It's all right. Everything is fine," Winston whispered, and the man shuffled into the alley. He looked half asleep.

Once he got up to them, Winston gently put a

hand on his shoulder and put the palm of his other hand in front of the policeman's face.

"Shhh."

The man's eyes closed, briefly reopened with sudden awareness, and then shut again. His features relaxed, and he slid down into a seated position, his back against the wall.

In another moment, he began to snore.

"Nice ability," Jaxon said.

"It comes in handy. I loathe violence. Let's make a move. It isn't safe here."

He led her to the other end of the alley, where it opened up into a street that had few pedestrians.

"We need you," Winston said.

"For what?"

"For your ability. That's why we've been searching for you all these years."

"Who's 'we'?"

"The Atlantis Guard. We protect our people's interests. This isn't the first time we've been persecuted, although this is by far the most dangerous challenge we've faced in generations."

"General Meade has created some sort of artificial Atlanteans," Jaxon said as the terrible image seared through her mind of Brett pushing against the storm of bullets.

"Oh dear, it's worse than we thought. But you can help. We have a team here, and we need you to find some of the old texts for us, some of the old places where our secret knowledge remains hidden. It's the only way to fight them."

They hurried along the nearly abandoned street, Winston in the lead.

"What kind of knowledge?"

"Secrets of healing, and of war. Sadly, we will need both if we have an army of our equals to contend with."

Jaxon had already found one of those secrets, but she didn't say that to Winston. This was all too new, she had too much to absorb, and she had been betrayed too many times by people claiming to want to help her for her to trust some random person on the street, even if he was one of her people.

"So where are we going to look?"

"We have some clues. I'm not the historian for this mission, but my colleague can tell you more. We have various places in the desert we need to check out. With your senses, you'll be of great help. You'll like the team. They can answer many questions you have about our people. It's sad that you grew up without a family, but you aren't the only one. Many of us are orphans, given up for our own safety. You can find a family among us."

A family. Winston sounded like he meant it. Despite his nervousness and the haste, they managed to get off of the street before getting spotted by the law again, his words came out gentle, caring. This guy knew what she had been through, and he had known her parents. She had a million questions to ask him.

But she already knew the two most important things—they had loved her, and they had believed in her.

"Almost there now," Winston said. "Once we meet the team, we can get out of Timbuktu and make straight for the Gambia, a few hundred miles south of here. That's the first place we need to look."

Jaxon stopped in her tracks. She was barely listening to Winston. Instead, she was thinking about what her parents had given her. She had thought that no one else had ever given her these things, but now she realized she was wrong.

Winston turned and called back to her. "Come on, we have to hurry. We can be in the Gambia by the end of the week. We'll be far away from all this trouble."

Jaxon slowly shook her head. "We can't go there. At least not yet."

Winston walked back to join her. "Why not?"

"You need to take me somewhere else first."

"Where?"

"Take me back to the Atlantis Allegiance," Jaxon said and paused. And when she said her next words, she knew she spoke the truth. "Take me back to my family."

CHAPTER 18

AUGUST 20, LOS ANGELES, CALIFORNIA

General Corbin sat in his hotel room in front of the television, laughing his head off at CNN. He used to hate watching television news. It was so superficial, so inaccurate. When you had top-secret access, you knew a lot more about what was really going on and realized that television news coverage was ninety-nine-point-nine percent wrong.

But now it was getting its facts wrong, according to his dictates.

The first phase of Operation Bicker had been a resounding success. That senator in Texas couldn't shake the KKK story Corbin's team had cooked up and had been hounded by questions and protests for weeks now. At a news conference, the senator had been interrupted by some Black Lives Matter protestors, and his patience had finally snapped. He'd called them "subhumans" and stormed off the stage.

Beautiful. No one remembered the fact that the senator had called a white guy on death row in Texas "subhuman" too; all the press covered was a rich white politician calling a bunch of black protestors less than human. His career was over.

So was the presidential bid of that congress-woman from New Hampshire. CNN had just aired that fake photo of her with the Russian mobster for the millionth time. The excuse this time was to analyze it on air to see if it was fake or real. It had been doctored well enough that CNN's "expert" said the results were inconclusive. Not that the jour-nalists at CNN cared. They knew that showing the photo was good for ratings, and people would go right on thinking what they were already thinking.

After that segment, they had a few talking heads babbling about her chances to secure her party's nomination for the next presidential election. General Corbin already knew the answer to that one. While she was putting on a brave and defiant face, the grapevine had told him that several rich donors had decided to withdraw their support from her campaign. She was sunk.

Operation Bicker was working like a charm. Now he could shift it into high gear and cause some real instability. He needed to get the two political parties into so much turmoil they would be paralyzed when he took power.

Project Poseidon was working like a charm too. Isadore's field report told him that Brett had become more independent and creative just before his death. So had good old General Meade, who had become enough of his former self again that he could resume his duties at the Pentagon. Of course, now he was still under Corbin's mental control. He would make a perfect spy in the Pentagon.

General Meade headed a team that oversaw operations in North Africa, so one of his first missions was to find out why the Russians were so interested in old Atlantean ruins. If the Russians were interested in any aspect of Atlantean history or culture, he had better check up on it. He would also have Meade check up on the reports that Mauritania had rounded up all the Atlanteans. Could the Russians be behind that, or some other group? If someone else was recruiting an Atlantean army, that could be a serious threat to his plans.

But for the moment, he could leave that in General Meade's capable hands. He was busy with the next phase of his plans.

The general chuckled at the news once more and turned it off. Although he wore his uniform, he was not in his office but rather in a hotel room in Los Angeles. He'd taken a couple of days of vacation to work on his own little side project. Leaving his room, he knocked on the door of a room down the hall. Dr. Jones came to the door carrying a medical bag. They hopped into a rented sedan with tinted windows and drove to a bad area of town for their appointment.

They pulled into the parking lot of a large church. It was an ugly thing, cheaply built, but clean, unlike most of the buildings in this trashy neighborhood. That showed self-respect and dignity, something so many Americans sadly lacked. Behind the church were two large prefab buildings. Teenagers lounged in the parking lot, drinking soda and smoking cigarettes. They stared at his uniform as he got out of the car. As he and the doctor walked to the front door of the church, they were followed by snorts of derision. He knew those were directed at his uniform.

He felt like snorting back. These kids didn't look like they had an ounce of respect in their bodies—not for him, not for their flag, not even for themselves.

He'd change that pretty quick.

The priest came to greet them at the door.

"Father Ryan, good to meet you," the general said, shaking his hand. The priest was an older man, his hair mostly turned to gray and his body a bit soft around the middle, but his handshake was firm and his eyes sharp. "This is my colleague, Dr. Jones. He's very interested in your operations as well."

"Ah yes!" Father Ryan said, shaking the doctor's hand. "I must thank you both for your generous contributions to Redemption House."

"We're only too happy to help," General Corbin said. "I've read fine things about your organization, and I'm always glad to support anyone who helps disadvantaged youth."

"The youth are the future of our nation," Father Ryan said.

You have no idea how right you are, General Corbin thought.

"So let me give you that tour I promised you on the phone," the priest said. "As you know, we accept any runaways who come to us, if they are under twenty-one. We don't ask questions, and we don't ask for identification. If we did, many would rather take their chances on the street. These kids have been hurt before, the system has failed them, and they want to remain anonymous. We respect that, feeling that the first priority is to get them away from the dangers of the street. Once they've settled in, we gently try to get them reintegrated back into society."

He led them through the church and to the dining hall, then to the separate boys' and girls' dorms. The priest introduced him to various members of staff, mostly volunteers, and explained that the kids could stay here as long as they liked if they followed the rules—no fighting, no drugs, curfew at nine p.m.

"Sadly, most drift away," Father Ryan said with a sigh. "Even this small amount of structure scares them off after a week or two. Most are chasing some sort of dream. Many come to Los Angeles thinking they'll get into the movies. That doesn't happen for most of them, of course, and those that do get into the movie industry don't end up in the kind of movies they were thinking about."

"What happens to the rest of them? Where do they go?" General Corbin asked.

The priest gave a tired shrug. "If they tell me, it's usually a lie. At least we give them a place to rest for a while, get cleaned up, and a chance to get off the streets. We're fighting against the tide here. Thousands of teenagers run away from home every year."

They entered the games room, a small room in the back of the church. A few teenagers were playing ping-pong, while others were busy with a game of Scrabble at a corner table.

"That ping-pong table looks a bit dilapidated," Dr. Jones said. "We'll have to fix that. And no Foosball? The kids need a Foosball table."

Father Ryan gave him a grateful smile. General Corbin smiled too. The good doctor was playing his part well.

"Shall we go get lunch and discuss what else we can do for Redemption House?" General Corbin asked.

"Oh, that's most kind," the priest said.

"I'll drive," General Corbin volunteered.

They went back to the parking lot. General Corbin got behind the wheel while Dr. Jones took the back seat, where his medical bag was hidden. Father Ryan took the front passenger's seat.

The doctor didn't wait long. As soon as they pulled out of the parking lot, he took a hypodermic needle from his bag and jabbed it into Father Ryan's neck.

"What the—" the priest managed to say before his eyelids hooded and his head slumped back on the seat.

"I do believe he was about to say 'hell,'" Dr. Jones said with a smile.

"Very unpriestly," General Corbin said. "So how long will it take to get him presentable?"

"We've improved the serum. Dr. Ziegler is waiting back at the hotel to give him an initial hypnotic session, and he'll stay here in LA to do follow-ups. We can call in to the church that he's taken ill and bring him home. He'll be ready to resume his duties in a couple of days. No one will be any the wiser."

"Good," the general said. "And once he's settled in, we'll have a steady supply of recruits."

"I'll get the team ready to open an LA office. We can start processing them by the end of the month."

"Get as many as you can, doctor. And once the system is up and running, give a few local physicians the same treatment we gave Father Ryan here. Then we can open branch offices in other places runaways gather—San Francisco and New York, for example. After that, we'll spread to other cities."

General Corbin had finally hit on the solution to his recruitment problem—teenaged runaways. There were thousands of them, and virtually no one gave a damn about them. Plus, since they were already missing, no one would notice if they disappeared. Illegal immigrants would be a good source too. He'd work on that later.

General Corbin smiled as he drove along the Los Angeles freeway back to his hotel. Things were looking up. Now that they had a workable serum, there was nothing to stop him from his rise to power.

As he drove up onto an overpass, the sprawl of Los Angeles stretched out to his left, reaching to the horizon. All that would be his one day—the city, the state, and eventually the country. And after that, who knew?

It would all be his.

ABOUT THE AUTHOR

S.A. Beck lives in sunny California. When she's not surfing, knitting or daydreaming in a hammock, she's writing novels. She is the author of *The Atlantis Saga* and *The Mage's Daughter Trilogy*.

sabeckbooks@gmail.com